HEROIC JUSTICE

HEROIC JUSTICE

M A COMLEY

2017

New York Times and USA Today bestselling author M A Comley
Published by Jeamel Publishing limited
Copyright © 2017 M A Comley
Digital Edition, License Notes

All rights reserved. This book or any portion thereof may not be reproduced, stored in a retrieval system, transmitted in any form or by any means electronic or mechanical, including photo-copying, or used in any manner whatsoever without the express written permission of the author, except for the use of brief quotations in a book review or scholarly journal.

This is a work of fiction. Names, characters, places and incidents are a product of the author's imagination or are used fictitiously, and any resemblance to actual persons living or dead, business establishments, events or locales is entirely coincidental.

ISBN-13: 978-1979456340

ISBN-10: 1979456348

OTHER BOOKS BY M A COMLEY

Blind Justice (Novella)
Cruel Justice (Book #1)
Mortal Justice (Novella)
Impeding Justice (Book #2)
Final Justice (Book #3)
Foul Justice (Book #4)
Guaranteed Justice (Book #5)
Ultimate Justice (Book #6)
Virtual Justice (Book #7)
Hostile Justice (Book #8)
Tortured Justice (Book #9)
Rough Justice (Book #10)
Dubious Justice (Book #11)
Calculated Justice (Book #12)
Twisted Justice (Book #13)
Justice at Christmas (Short Story)
Prime Justice (Book #14)
Heroic Justice (Book #15)
Unfair Justice (a 10,000 word short story coming June 2017)
Clever Deception (co-written by Linda S Prather)
Tragic Deception (co-written by Linda S Prather)
Sinful Deception (co-written by Linda S Prather)
Forever Watching You (DI Miranda Carr thriller)
Wrong Place (DI Sally Parker thriller #1)
No Hiding Place (DI Sally Parker thriller #2)
Cold Case (DI Sally Parker #3)
Deadly Encounter (DI Sally Parker thriller series #4)
Web of Deceit (DI Sally Parker Novella with Tara Lyons)

The Caller (co-written with Tara Lyons)
Evil In Disguise – a novel based on True events
Deadly Act (Hero series novella)
Torn Apart (Hero series #1)
End Result (Hero series #2)
In Plain Sight (Hero Series #3)
Double Jeopardy (Hero Series #4 Due out in July 2017)
Sole Intention (Intention series #1)
Grave Intention (Intention series #2)
Devious Intention (Intention #3)
Merry Widow (A Lorne Simpkins short story)
It's A Dog's' Life (A Lorne Simpkins short story)
A Time To Heal (A Sweet Romance)
A Time For Change (A Sweet Romance)
High Spirits
The Temptation series (Romantic Suspense/New Adult Novellas)
Past Temptation (available now)
Lost Temptation (available now)

Keep in touch with the author at:

Twitter
https://twitter.com/Melcom1

Blog
http://melcomley.blogspot.com

Facebook
http://smarturl.it/sps7jh

Newsletter
http://smarturl.it/8jtcvv

BookBub
www.bookbub.com/authors/m-a-comley

ACKNOWLEDGMENTS

Thank you as always to my rock, Jean, who keeps me supplied with endless cups of coffee while I punish my keyboard. I'd be lost without you in my life.

Special thanks as always go to my talented editor, Stefanie Spangler Buswell and to Karri Klawiter for her superb cover design expertise.

My heartfelt thanks go to my wonderful proofreader Joseph for spotting all the lingering nits.

Thank you to Dee and Kelly from my ARC group for allowing me to use your names.

And finally, to all the wonderful Bloggers and Facebook groups for their never-ending support of my work.

M A Comley

PROLOGUE

He slid into the alley and pulled a mask and mirror from his bag. As he fixed the expensively made latex mask in place with the aid of the mirror, his breath was ragged, and his heartbeat escalated. He'd gone over every intricate detail of the plan until the images were imprinted on his eyelids when he closed his eyes at night, not that he'd slept much in the last week. He edged closer to the cinema's alley exit then waited for it to open. He checked his watch—the first afternoon screening would end at any moment. The second the door opened, he would be in there, faster than Usain Bolt, ready for the next phase.

The click of the fire exit door alerted him just before a stream of people left the cinema, all laughing and dissecting the film they'd just seen. There were more punters in there than he'd anticipated. Would there be as many for the next sitting, he wondered. Clenching and unclenching his fists helped relieve the tension that had just enveloped him. He inched his way sideways towards the door, and after the final person left, he grabbed the door before it closed.

Concealed behind the long red velour drapes covering the entrance, he waited until the theatre filled again. Then he walked up and down the aisles, searching for his target as he listened to the voices. Within seconds he had the man on his radar and chose a spot a few seats away in the row behind him. The man was alone.

Five minutes later, the lights dipped and the commercials began. For once, he was glad the volume was deafening. He slipped into the seat directly behind the man. After a few minutes, he pulled a pen knife from his pocket. During a particularly noisy part of the advert, he flicked it open.

His saliva dried up, and he swallowed. With a shaking hand, he reached forward. In one swift movement, the knife dug deep into the man's throat, and his head lolled to the side. He wiped the knife on the man's jacket and sat there for a few moments longer until his heart rate slowed down to near normal. His first kill under his belt, he allowed himself to smile; a broad smile of satisfaction that pulled at his thin lips beneath the mask.

As the titles for the main film rolled up on the screen, he left his seat and parked himself at the end of the row, close to the emergency exit. When the usherette walked past him, he slid behind the curtain once more. Again, he waited for a noisy part in the movie that would disguise his next move, which would certainly set off the alarm. A girl screamed on the big screen, and the soundtrack increased in tempo, concealing the sound of the alarm when he pushed open the exit door. In the alley, he slammed the door shut behind him to silence the alarm. He escaped the alley before anyone could check what, or who, had set off the alarm.

He merged into the flow of pedestrians moving towards his car, which was parked a few streets away.

Reaching his car, he ripped off his mask, tucked it away in the carrier bag, threw it in the backseat and breathed a relieved sigh. He'd accomplished the perfect crime. *And this is just the beginning...*

CHAPTER ONE

Lorne was flabbergasted by the news her daughter, Charlie, had just shared with her and her husband, Tony, over the breakfast table. Lately, they rarely got the chance to share any kind of meal together, but as it was Lorne's forty-eighth birthday, they'd made an exception. She was feeling her age, especially after Charlie's surprise announcement.

"It's entirely up to you, love. I have to say when you started talking, I thought you were going to say that you were pregnant. I'm so relieved about that. I'm too young to become a grandmother." She laughed when she saw the colour rise in her daughter's cheeks.

"Grant me with some sense, Mum. I'm not even sure I want kids yet. Brandon and I want to see the world a bit before we settle down. You know, do all the things that you missed out on by having me so early."

Tony chuckled and placed his hand over Lorne's. "Consider yourself told, Mummy dearest."

She turned to him, wide-eyed and lost for words, for a change.

Charlie leapt out of her seat, hugged her mother, and planted a soppy wet kiss on her cheek. "You know I didn't mean it like that. But kids really aren't on my agenda, not for a long time anyway."

"Glad to hear it. You know I love you more than life itself, and I have never regretted having you, but I do think I should have waited until I was in my thirties before starting a family. I admire you for wanting to have a career first, love."

"You don't know how pleased I am to hear you say that, Mum. I was scared you'd throw me out after sharing my news."

Lorne's mouth gaped open and closed immediately. "What? Why on earth would I want to kick you out? Tony and I love having you here with us."

Charlie's gaze dropped to the table. "Well, I do think that sometimes I should give you guys some space. You've been married, what?

Eight or nine years now, and you've always had me hanging around your necks. I'm trying hard to save up for a place of my own, but you know how expensive property is around here."

Lorne shook her head. "Never, never think you've outstayed your welcome, love. I don't think I'm out of place speaking for both of us when I say that we adore having you around."

"If only to care for the dogs," Tony said, his eyes glistening with devilment.

Both Lorne and Charlie slapped him on the arm. "That's not true, and you know it, Agent Boy." Lorne knew using the nickname he detested would wipe the smile from his face.

"Okay, I'm suitably chastised, ladies. You know you'll always have a home here with us, Charlie. Never think you're in our way. I know I don't say this much, but I sincerely love you as if I'd spawned you myself."

Lorne tutted. "Jesus, Tony. There's got to be a better way of wording that. What my darling husband is trying to say is that he regards you as his flesh and blood."

Tony winked and tapped the side of his nose. "You've got it. Your mum is right, Charlie. To me, you're the daughter I've never had and not likely to have, given your mother's age."

Lorne placed her head in her hands and roared with laughter. Removing her hands, she wiped away the tears running down her cheeks. "Crikey, hit an old girl in the solar plexus when she's feeling her age, why don't ya?"

Tony blew her a kiss. "Nonsense. You look as stunning now as you did in your twenties. I've seen the photos. I overlook the crow's feet just as much as you ignore my wrinkles and grey hair. I wouldn't have you any other way, love of my life."

Lorne turned to Charlie. "That's as romantic as he gets. I think there's a compliment hidden in that statement somewhere."

Charlie laughed and shook her head. "I hope Brandon and I will be as happy as you guys are when we finally settle down." She raised her hands. "Don't go building your hopes up just yet—that's years away. We're happy as we are right now and don't see the point in spoiling it. I'm not like the soppy girls my age who buy all the wedding magazines and constantly dream about walking down the aisle. I've got my head screwed on. I want a career first, and then everything else will slot into place nicely, I hope."

"It will, love. You're doing the right thing. Okay, we've gone off track a little somewhere along the line. So, you've signed up to join the force and had your acceptance letter. What's next?"

"In what respect, Mum?"

"Well, in my day, we had to attend Hendon for a seventeen-week training course. I heard that all changed back in 2007. I've lost touch with things these days. What are new recruits expected to do now?"

"It's pretty much the same. It's an eighteen-week course. Though, nowadays, it's called the Peel Centre, although everyone still calls it Hendon, I'm led to believe."

"Is that so? You live and learn as they say."

"I reckon most of the training takes place on the job, though, right?"

"It does that, love. I remember having a whale of a time at Hendon. Upon reflection, maybe we had too much of a good time. You'll love it there, I'm sure."

"It'll still be hard work—don't ever take the training lightly," Tony piped up. "Although I always maintain it's better to learn the day-to-day things in situ. There's only a limited number of things instructors can teach to prepare you for what goes on in the real world."

Lorne motioned with her head in his direction. "Hark at him. That might be how MI6 train their staff—you know, where anything goes—but in the force, there are certain procedures and laws that need to be adhered to, Tony."

"I'm not disputing that, Wise Owl. It's the same in any career. On-the-job training is definitely the way forward."

Charlie nodded. "I don't mind. Think I'd prefer it that way. It was the one thing that prevented me from signing up at eighteen, if I'm honest. Hated the thought of having to sit in a classroom for months on end, going over the same things, until the way the force *expects* us to react to certain situations was drilled into us."

"You'll fit in better now that you're older and wiser. I'm so proud of you, sweetheart. I wonder where you'll be based."

"No idea. They don't tell you that until the final day of the course, I think. We have one hurdle to tackle before I enrol, Mum. What's going to happen to this place?"

Lorne and Charlie both glanced in Tony's direction. He raised his hands in front of him. "Whoa... now wait just a minute. If you think I'm going back to running this place, you can think again. I have a very busy private investigation business to run, remember?"

"I'm not saying full time, just in the interim. I'll have a word with Carol, see if she can up her hours around here for a few weeks until I find someone suitable to take over."

"You know I'll do what I can to help out, but the business is growing monthly. I'd hate to stop the momentum now. Joe and I have struggled to build our clientele over the last few years, and I'd rather not do anything that might put all our hard work in jeopardy."

"I appreciate that, love. We're all going to pitch in when we can, right, Charlie?"

"Of course, Mum. Why don't I ask down at the dog agility club Brandon and I belong to? Maybe someone down there will be able to point us in the right direction. It's a cushy job for the right person."

"It is, but my main priority is ensuring the dogs are well cared for and exercised properly. I know some places are just happy to leave the dogs in their cages all day and just clear up the mess. I really don't want us to be tarred with the same brush. We've worked hard to build our reputation over the years; it would be a shame if someone came along and spoilt that in a matter of weeks."

"We'll make sure that doesn't happen, Mum."

"Hey, if you want, I can rig up the kennels with cameras." Tony grinned.

"I know you're joking about that, but I think it might be a good idea, at least until we're sure we can trust the person we employ," Lorne agreed.

Charlie chewed her lip. "Is that wise? It's a bit like Big Brother is watching you, isn't it?"

"Hmm... I understand what you mean, love, but our main concern has to be the welfare of the dogs. I've seen so many horrendous things on the internet lately regarding pet parlours and boarding kennels, that I don't think we can ever be over-cautious about who we employ or their ongoing treatment of the dogs."

"I know, Mum. It's a tough one. I'll ask around the agility group. Those guys wouldn't recommend anyone dodgy to me. They wouldn't dare—everyone knows whose daughter I am." Charlie winked at her and smiled.

Lorne chuckled. "Glad my reputation precedes me. It's good to keep people on their toes. Right, I must finish this then shoot. Can I leave you two to clear up?"

Tony and Charlie exchanged amused looks.

"Don't you always? Birthday or no birthday!" Tony chided playfully.

Lorne ate the last mouthful of bacon, dropped her knife and fork on the plate, and rose from the table. She ruffled Sheba's head and kissed her on the nose. "I'll see you all later. Have a good day."

"You, too, Mum. Hope they don't give you the bumps at the station."

"Blimey! I hope they don't, either. Haven't had those since I was thirteen. I wonder if that birthday tradition would be classed as bullying nowadays." She shuddered at the humiliation she had endured one year when a group of boys from her class had set upon her at the local park on the way home from school, flung her in the air, and kicked her on the way down before they dropped her on the wet grass. Her dad had been furious and demanded action from the headmistress the next day. But as the incident had taken place outside the school gates and was deemed a harmless tradition, the head had refused to get involved. That humiliation had lived with Lorne for a few months until she sought out her own retribution on the culprits. The four boys concerned never bothered her again, thankfully.

Lorne drove into work, her mind full of the conversation her family had discussed over breakfast. She knew one person who would be thrilled to learn of Charlie's decision to join the force: her partner, Katy, who had not long returned to work after maternity leave.

She pulled into the car park, and moments later, Katy drew up alongside her. Lorne smiled at her partner and noticed how tired she looked. "Hey, everything all right with Georgina?"

"Yeah, I suppose so. I only managed to get a few hours' sleep, though. Happy birthday." Katy leaned forward, pecked Lorne on the cheek then produced a pretty pink gift bag.

Narrowing her eyes, Lorne shook her head. "Thanks. I thought I told you not to bother with a present. I'd rather you spent the money on that adorable goddaughter of mine, or soon to be, should I say. Are you looking forward to the christening do?"

Katy sighed heavily and puffed out her cheeks. "Yes and no. AJ is still having problems with his parents—nothing new there—and now Mum is saying that Dad has something major going on at work, and they might not be able to come down for it. Why the hell do families have to cause so much shit?"

Lorne rubbed Katy's arm. "I'm sorry, love. Maybe just lay it on the line with them. If they can't drop everything to attend their own granddaughter's one and only christening, then shame on them. Nothing, and I mean nothing, would get in the way of Tony and me, or Charlie for that matter, attending the special day."

"That's a relief to hear, especially as you and Tony are going to be her godparents."

Lorne chuckled. "There is that, but you know what I mean. If we had something major going on, we'd postpone it in favour of the christening, and we're not even related. Where the heck do your parents get off?"

"I know. The thing I hate the most is the amount of friction it's causing between AJ and me."

"Don't let them win, love. Ignore them if you can. My lot will ensure the day is a success, I can guarantee that." Lorne opened the bag and pulled out a bottle of Cool Water perfume. Her eyes misted up. It was her favourite because her ex-partner, Pete, used to wear the cologne of the same brand, and the smell still lingered in the doorway to her office now and again.

"You daft mare. Don't go breaking down on me now."

Lorne sniffed. "You know what this stuff means to me. Thank you, that's so thoughtful. You're a treasure."

They walked through the entrance of the station. The desk sergeant Mick Crawford greeted them with a smile and handed Lorne a birthday card. She was touched by the kind gesture. "Thanks, Mick, you're very kind."

"Let's hope the day doesn't turn out to be too hectic for you, ma'am. I sense differently, though, from the message I left on your desk this morning."

"Sounds ominous. Want to give us a hint?"

"Nasty death in a cinema, ma'am."

"Did I hear something on the news about that last night?"

"Possibly, happened yesterday afternoon."

Lorne frowned. "How come I'm only hearing about it now, Mick?"

He looked over his shoulder and leaned in closer. "Not sure really, ma'am, but I knew you'd want to hear about it first thing."

"Thanks. We better go take a look, Katy."

Lorne spotted the note on her desk a few minutes later. She paused in the doorway of her office a little longer than normal. *Is it my imagination, or is the smell of Pete's aftershave even stronger today?*

"Are you here, mate?" she whispered. She scanned the room looking for any kind of response, and her heart skipped a beat when the blind at the top of the window fluttered. A true cynic would have said that was because of the breeze, except the window wasn't even open. Her lips parted in a broad smile, and she made her way over to the desk to pick up the note the desk sergeant had delivered earlier. She left the office again to find Katy.

"Fancy a trip to the mortuary? We can call at the scene on the way over there."

"Do we have time for a quick coffee first?"

"Sure. Mine's a white with one sugar, in case you've forgotten."

Katy shook her head. "I suppose I walked into that one. I'll bring it in to you. Do you have much post to deal with? I know you like to get that out of the way first thing."

"Enough. I bet you don't miss that part of the job, eh?"

"Nope. I used to detest it when I was in your position."

Lorne nodded and went back to her office. She still felt a little awkward filling Katy's shoes. However, it had been Katy's decision to ask for a demotion once she'd found out she was pregnant. DCI Roberts hadn't hesitated in appointing Lorne back to DI, not that he'd had the decency to consult her before he'd announced it to the rest of the team. Surprisingly, she had returned to the role easily enough and not looked back. It had probably been more relaxed for her when Katy was on maternity leave, but she couldn't see there being any significant problems between them now.

A quick flick through the post and Lorne was done for the day, regarding the admin side of things at least. She finished her coffee and tapped Katy on the shoulder as she breezed through the incident room. "Ready, partner? Guys, finish up the paperwork to the two cases we've just dealt with. That'll leave you clear to concentrate on this case once we have all the facts to hand."

Katy drank her coffee while the rest of the team put their heads down and got on with their work.

When they arrived at the cinema, around twenty minutes later, the area was cordoned off with crime scene tape. Lorne and Katy showed their IDs then dipped underneath the tape. A man in his late forties to early fifties was lingering inside the doorway, pacing up and down, looking severely stressed.

"Are you the manager?" Lorne asked, flashing her warrant card at him.

"Thank God! I've been standing around, wondering when someone in authority was going to show up. Head office are doing their nuts. They're on the phone every half an hour, demanding to know when the cinema can open its doors again. What can I tell them, Inspector?"

"I'm sorry, I didn't catch your name."

"Jonathon Wallace."

"Mr. Wallace, it really depends what the Scenes of Crime Officers find. You're aware that all the evidence needs to be collected from the crime scene before we can declare the area free to use again?"

"Yes, I'm aware. But head office is on my case and piling on the pressure."

"Would you like me to have a word with someone for you?"

He blew out a juddering breath. "That would be great if you could. I get the impression they think I'm pulling a fast one."

"Get me the number, and my partner will put them in the picture." Lorne turned to Katy as if seeking her approval. Katy shrugged and nodded.

Wallace handed Katy a card then showed Lorne through the main doors of the theatre where the crime had occurred. Katy walked away, in search of a more private spot to place the call.

"Would you mind telling us what happened?" Lorne asked.

He sighed. "Like I told the uniformed officers last night, one of my girls found the man sitting in his seat. She shook him on the shoulder, thinking that he'd fallen asleep during the film, and his head slipped to the side. She screamed when she saw the amount of blood pouring from his throat. She hadn't noticed it before his head moved."

"Do you know how long the man had been sitting there?"

"Marjorie, the attendant, said that everyone left the theatre after the first show, so it's not like he'd been there that long. A maximum of two hours, I guess."

Katy returned and said, "All done. That should keep them off your back for the rest of the day. I told them this place would be treated as a crime scene for at least twenty-four to forty-eight hours."

A spot of colour appeared in the manager's ashen cheeks. "Thank you, you'll never know how much I appreciate that."

Heroic Justice

Lorne surveyed the area. "No cameras in here, I suppose?"

"In the foyer, yes, but not in here. Why would anyone do such a thing to a fellow human being?"

"That's what we intend to find out, sir. We'll need to speak to Marjorie if she's on duty."

"She is. I told her to take the day off, but she insisted coming in today, said she would only sit at home, going over the events in her mind otherwise."

"So you called the police right away?"

"Of course. As soon as I saw the man and realised he was dead. Not sure how I managed to punch in the numbers; my hands were shaking so much. What happens now?"

Lorne looked along the line of seats. SOCO had placed a couple of markers in the area. Just as she thought all officers had left the scene, she spotted one of the technicians heading their way from the rear.

"I asked this area to be kept clear. You should know better than to approach the scene without wearing the appropriate attire, Inspector."

"Sorry, Ted. We didn't get too close, I promise." She turned to face Mr. Wallace and dismissed him. "We'll have a word with the technician and come and find you in a few minutes, sir."

The manager walked back out to the foyer, his shoulders slumped in despair.

"We're almost finished here. Can't tell you much, Inspector, apart from it looks like the victim was attacked from behind with some kind of knife. The pathologist will be able to tell you more if you contact her directly."

"Thanks, we're just on our way over there now, thought we'd drop by to survey the scene and question the staff first."

Lorne and Katy left the theatre and found Wallace in the foyer, chatting with a busty blonde in her thirties. Wallace saw them approach and took a few paces away from the woman. Lorne recognised the signs of guilt and put it down to the couple having an illicit affair.

"Are you Marjorie?"

The blonde nodded. "I am. I found the poor man. Haven't slept a wink all night."

"Sorry about that. Is there somewhere we can have a quick chat, to get a brief statement from you?"

"You can use my office," Wallace suggested, pointing at a door on the right.

"Thanks, shall we?" Lorne led the way, and Katy brought up the rear.

"Please, try not to be nervous. We just need to be sure of all the facts before beginning our investigation properly."

"I'm not sure I can tell you much. The theatre was empty, except for the dead man. Sorry, that was insensitive of me—the victim. It's my job to ensure everyone leaves before the next show begins. I approached the man and shook his shoulder. It took a while for my eyes to adjust after just turning on the main lights. I screamed when I saw his throat had been cut." She removed a tissue from her jacket pocket and dabbed her eyes. "I've never seen a dead person before. I know some people get off on such things, but I just found the whole thing rather distressing. Do you think I'll ever have another decent night's sleep again?"

"I'm sure you will. I'm so sorry you've had such a dreadful experience. Tell me, during the movie, did you walk around the theatre at all?"

The woman sniffed and then blew her nose. "Yes, I have to go in there before the main film starts, to sell ice cream to the punters."

"Do you remember going near the victim during that time?"

"Yes, I stood alongside him for a few moments before I moved over to the next aisle."

Lorne raised a hopeful eyebrow. "Did you see anyone sitting in the seat behind the victim?"

The woman's brow furrowed as she thought. "I can't recall seeing anyone."

"The victim, did he buy an ice cream from you?"

"No. He didn't. No one in that aisle did. It was a very slow day."

"Did he acknowledge you at all? A smile perhaps?"

"I don't think so."

"Okay, I'm just trying to establish when he was killed. Did you notice anything odd about him?"

"Nothing. He was just staring at the screen, even though there was nothing playing at the time. Oh, God, do you think he could have been dead then?"

"I'm not sure. What time did the film finish?"

"About five or thereabouts. That's when I tapped him on the shoulder and saw he was covered in blood and had a gaping wound on his neck. His eyes were wide open. I screamed, and the manager arrived and whisked me away. He was just as shocked as me."

"It must have been a terrible blow for you. During the film, what do you do?"

Marjorie looked puzzled by the question, so Lorne elucidated for her. "Do you remain in the theatre at all times, at the customers' beck and call, or do you go elsewhere?"

"Oh, I see. I generally drift between the foyer and the theatre. I usually linger at the back, wouldn't want to be accused of getting in the way at all."

"Did you happen to glance at the victim during the film? Perhaps you saw someone sitting behind him at some point during the course of the movie?"

"No, I can't remember that at all. I'm useless. I'm not being obstructive on purpose, I promise. I just didn't see anything. I'd willingly tell you if I had."

"Please, don't upset yourself. You're doing well. I have to ask these questions in case it jolts your memory."

"I understand. I wish I could tell you more. It's so frustrating for me. I want to see this hateful person caught quickly, I can assure you."

"As do we. During the film, did anyone leave early?"

"Gosh, lots of people walk past me all the time on their way to the loo."

"Perhaps you noticed someone who didn't return to their seat after nipping to the loo?"

She shook her head. "Nope, I'm a people watcher. I would have noticed if someone had gone in to the loo and not returned. I would have checked on them in case they'd suffered an accident in the toilet. Again, that's part of my job, to remain vigilant."

"Is there a possibility that the culprit found another exit to use in that case?"

Marjorie's eyes narrowed, then she hit her head with the heel of her hand. "Shit! Why didn't it occur to me before this? The alarm to the emergency exit went off for the briefest time during the film. I rushed to see what the problem was, but by the time I arrived, the door was closed, and the alarm had stopped. I put it down to a technical glitch."

Lorne and Katy glanced at each other, their interest piqued. "Does that type of thing often happen?"

"No, very rarely, if I'm honest."

"And where is this door situated?"

"Close to where the victim was found."

Lorne clicked her fingers. "Katy, nip and tell the SOCO guys to examine the door thoroughly, will you?"

Katy rose from the chair and rushed out of the room.

Marjorie gasped and placed her hand over her mouth. "You think that's how he escaped?"

"It's possible, not something I'm willing to rule out at this time. Is there anything else you can think of that might possibly help with our enquiries?"

"I really can't think of anything. Maybe I can take a contact number and get in touch if anything comes to mind."

Lorne slid a business card across the desk. "Call me day or night. I'm always available."

"That's very kind of you. Sorry I can't be of any further help."

"Nonsense, you've been very helpful. Please, try not to dwell on this too much, and for goodness' sake, don't feel guilty about the demise of this man."

"Thank you. I'll try not to, but then I keep thinking what if I could have saved him. Maybe he suffered in his seat for a long time before he finally died."

"That's unlikely, given the extensive wound he suffered. In my experience, his death would have been instantaneous."

Lorne followed the woman out of the room and into the foyer, where Katy was talking to the manager.

"We'll go now. One last question, if I may? I don't suppose there's any form of CCTV on that emergency exit, is there?"

The manager's eyes bulged. "Why yes, yes, there is. Two seconds, and I'll get the disc sorted for you."

Lorne and Katy paced the area while Marjorie went into the office with Mr. Wallace. They reappeared a few minutes later. The manager handed Lorne the disc case. "That's the view of the door. I spotted a person of interest—I think that's the right term the police use."

Lorne smiled. "Wonderful, I'll get one of my team on it right away. Thanks for your assistance. Marjorie has my number, if you think of anything else that might be of interest and help the case progress." Lorne shook Mr. Wallace's hand before she and Katy rushed out of the building and into the car.

"To the lab or back to the station?" Katy asked, strapping herself in.

"I'll get Graham on this first, and then we'll shoot over to see Patti," Lorne replied, adrenaline pumping through her system. She had a good feeling about this.

However, Lorne's interest in what was on that disc kept them at the station longer than anticipated. Graham whizzed through the disc and stopped at the man slipping in through the door. His head was bowed as though he was intentionally avoiding any CCTV cameras. It was impossible to make out any distinguishing features from that viewpoint. Graham skipped through the disc footage again to locate the same man emerging from the cinema's emergency exit and slamming the door swiftly behind him. This time, his face was in full view.

"His face looks kind of weird, or is that my imagination?" She leaned closer to the screen. "Is that a bloody mask he's wearing?" Lorne slapped her hand against her thigh. "Shit!"

"Looks like it to me. Well, that's dampened our enthusiasm in one swift movement," Katy replied, sighing.

"Okay. What's done is done. Let's not dwell on the negatives. Come on, Katy, we have a meeting of minds to attend with Patti."

CHAPTER TWO

"Hello, girls. You're later than I anticipated. Everything all right?" Patti, the pathologist, asked.

Lorne screwed her nose up at her good friend. "After calling in at the scene, we got excited by the CCTV footage the manager of the cinema gave us. But it turned out to be useless. It highlighted the culprit, all right. However, he was wearing a damn disguise. Some kind of latex mask, I suspect."

"Damn! Not so good. Was there anything you could use from it?"

"Nope, I don't think so. It was hard to judge what height he is or even if he's actually a male. Once we've established from where the culprit had escaped, we asked the SOCO technicians to examine the door for us. I suppose we'll have to see what comes back from that. It was difficult to tell if he was wearing gloves from the image we saw."

Patti crossed her fingers. "We live in hope. Right, I have a corpse sitting in my fridge that you should see."

"Did you find any form of ID on him?" Lorne asked as they followed Patti down the hallway and into the huge refrigerated area.

Patti pulled out the steel drawer to reveal the victim's body, concealed by a white sheet. "I have his personal effects for you, and yes, there was an ID. Ladies, say hello to Gary Ross." Patti folded back the sheet to reveal the man who appeared to be in his late thirties. He had handsome features, bright blue eyes, and reddish-blonde hair. The opening in his throat, although Patti had stitched it, drew Lorne's eye immediately.

"Poor man. By the looks of things, I think we're talking about a random attack," Lorne said.

"I'm not sure how you've come to that conclusion, boss," Katy replied, gagging a little.

Patti nodded. "I'm inclined to agree with you, Lorne, given the evidence. This was a vicious attack, an intense attack, but also a cowardly one. If the culprit had known the victim, I think he would have confronted Mr. Ross from the front and not the back. Pure speculation on my part, of course."

"I agree, Patti. So, where do we go from here? I take it there was no other DNA or weapon found at the scene?"

"Nothing has come to light as yet, Lorne. I'll give you his details, as I'm sure his wife must be going out of her mind with worry."

"Wife?"

"He was wearing a thick wedding band."

"Bugger. Okay, then that will have to be our next stop. Why the heck hasn't someone chased his ID up already? Bloody amateurs!"

Patti covered the victim's face again and pushed the corpse back into the refrigerator. In silence, Lorne and Katy followed Patti to her office.

After Patti wrote down the man's address, Lorne and Katy headed over to break the news to the victim's wife.

"Why would someone choose their victim randomly, like that?" Katy asked, her thumb and forefinger on her chin as she spoke.

Lorne started the car then glanced her way. "I always see it as cowardice. I think it's the worst crime going. To not know anything about that person, whether they're married or have children or not, it really is the pits to me. It also makes our job a lot harder. We're going to have to ask the wife and his boss, if he has one, the normal questions, but the answers are just going to tick us off and frustrate the life out of us."

"Nothing new there then."

Twenty-five minutes later, Lorne drew up outside a large detached house in a beautiful tree-lined street. "Nice house. Must cost a pretty penny, too, in this affluent area."

"Which makes me wonder what he was doing frequenting the cinema during the day."

Lorne chewed the inside of her mouth for a second. "Maybe it was his day off, his guilty pleasure to escape a busy lifestyle and spend some time alone doing something he loved. I don't know. I can't remember the last time I went to the cinema, if I'm honest. I think I overdosed on seeing *Grease* when I was a youngster."

"Overdosed? How?"

"I saw the film five times in a week. I know. Don't think bad of me—I was a teenager in love with John Travolta. Oh, heck, now I've got that blasted song rattling around my mind. 'You're the one that I want... oo... oo... oo, honey.'"

Katy sniggered. "Thanks for that. Now I'm not going to be able to bloody shift it from my head, either."

"Serious faces now. Let's go break the news to the man's wife."

The gravel crunched beneath their feet as they approached the front door of the double-fronted house. There was no car on the drive, but a single garage was situated off to the left. Lorne rang the doorbell and smiled at Katy as they waited for Mrs. Ross to answer.

"Hello?" a smartly dressed lady said from the pavement outside the property. "I don't think anyone is at home."

Lorne and Katy walked back towards the woman.

"Any idea where they are?" Lorne asked, showing the woman her ID.

"Pauline is away on a management course for work, and I'm not sure where Gary is. I haven't seen him since yesterday afternoon. Not that I'm one of those nosy parkers. I'm part of the neighbourhood watch scheme. We look out for each other on this street. Not many inhabitants of London can say that these days."

"Glad to hear it. I don't suppose you have a contact number for Pauline?"

"I have indeed. Is there something wrong?"

"We need to contact her regarding her husband, that's all."

"I'll be right back." The woman rushed into her house next door and emerged with her address book within seconds. "Here you go. I brought a pen for you just in case."

Lorne punched the number directly into her mobile phone. "Thank you, that's brilliant. Katy, can you take the lady's details down for me please?" She left the two women and returned to the Ross's front doorstep to place the call. The phone was answered on the first ring. "Hello, Mrs. Pauline Ross?"

"Yes," she whispered.

"I'm so sorry to disturb you. I wouldn't do it if it wasn't urgent. Do you have time for a chat?"

"If I have to. One minute, I'm just leaving a meeting."

Lorne heard a chair scraping and a man's abrupt voice sounding displeased when Pauline announced she had to leave the room. "Are you there?" Lorne asked.

The woman tutted. "Yes, now who are you?"

Heroic Justice

"I'm sorry to have reached you at such an inconvenient time. I'm Detective Inspector Lorne Warner."

"The police? What on earth...?"

"Where are you, Pauline?"

"I'm in Cheshire at present. Why? What's this about, Inspector?"

Lorne deliberated whether to tell the woman about her husband's demise over the phone or not and decided against it. "Sorry, I'm going to have to insist that you come back home as soon as possible. Can you do that?"

"Really? My course is due to finish today. I'll be home later this evening. Will that do?"

"I'd prefer it if it were sooner, but it will have to do. What time do you anticipate being home this evening?"

"We're supposed to be having an end-of-course dinner. I was going to drive home after that, but if it's urgent, then I can skip the meal. Please, what is this about?"

"I'd rather tell you when you get here. You have my number. Can you ring me later to give me an idea of what time you'll be arriving, and I'll be here to greet you?"

"It sounds serious. Have you spoken to Gary, my husband?"

Lorne clenched and unclenched her free hand. The last thing she wanted was to share the bad news over the phone and cause the woman to have an accident during her drive back home. "No, I haven't spoken to him. Drive carefully, and I'll see you later."

"Okay. I'm not happy that you're keeping me in the dark, though."

"Trust me. You're not in any trouble. However, it is urgent that I speak to you in person. See you soon."

"If I can get away earlier, I will."

"I appreciate that. Goodbye, drive safely." Lorne disconnected the call and returned to Katy and the neighbour. "Mrs. Ross will be on her way home as soon as she can get away. It was the final day of her course anyway."

"Good. May I ask what this is about, Inspector?"

"I'm afraid I can't tell you that until I've spoken to Mrs. Ross. You said you saw Gary yesterday?"

"Yes, in the afternoon, around lunchtime. Is he in trouble? Come to think of it, I don't recall seeing him return to the house last night. Has he been arrested? Is that it?"

"No. I'm sorry. I really can't divulge what has happened until I speak with his wife. Thank you for your help, Mrs...?"

"Groocock. Silly name, I know."

Lorne smiled. "Thank you for all your help, Mrs. Groocock. We'll be in touch soon if we need any further details from you."

Looking dejected, the woman returned to her house and closed the door quietly behind her.

"Yikes, I thought she was going to keep grilling us until one of us broke down," Katy admitted.

Lorne motioned for them to get in the car. "I love the idea of neighbourhood watch, but it does bring out the Agatha Christies in the world. She means well, I suppose. We'll go back to the station, and I'll return this evening before going home. It could be a late one."

"Want me to tag along? I don't mind."

"No, you get home to AJ and Georgina. He'll need the respite after a long day with a crying baby."

They both laughed as the car pulled away from the kerb. When they arrived back at the station, Lorne asked the team to find out all the background information they could about the Ross's. As far as Lorne was concerned, the rest of the day dragged by and involved a lot of paper pushing and mundane office chores. She was relieved when her mobile rang at five o'clock. "DI Warner."

"Hello, Inspector, this is Pauline Ross. I'm not far from home if you have time in your busy schedule to meet me."

Lorne didn't detect any sarcasm in the woman's tone, despite her words. "Okay, I'm on my way over to your place now. See you in a little while."

She ended the call and unhooked her jacket from the back of the chair. She always felt the need to dress appropriately when on duty, even when the weather was a little sticky. "Right, gang, I'm going over to see the victim's wife. I'll continue home from there. Get off when you're ready, and we'll have a meeting first thing about what we should do next."

~ ~ ~

When Lorne arrived at the Ross's house, Pauline was unloading the car. "Can I help you with that, Pauline?"

"Inspector Warner, I take it?"

"Please, call me Lorne."

Together, they ferried the woman's suitcase, laptop and several high-class boutique bags into the hallway and placed them at the bottom of the stairs. The house, although very impressive on the exterior, was very warm and cosy on the inside, where subtle browns and creams had been used to create the tranquil ambience. Pauline led Lorne through to the amazing extension at the rear.

"Wow, this is beautiful. What a stunning room." The back wall consisted of glass from floor to ceiling, and the four skylights in the sloping ceiling flooded the room with extra light. The kitchen had a bank of full-length units, which included three ovens, one of which Lorne suspected was a microwave and a super-duper coffee machine. She really was envious of the beautifully designed kitchen, which she suspected would have cost well over fifty thousand to install.

"Thank you. We had it fitted last year. I spend most of my time out here now. Can I get you a coffee?"

Lorne's eyes were drawn to the built-in coffee machine. "One of those?"

Pauline laughed. "Yes, I haven't quite mastered it yet. Will ordinary filter coffee do?"

"Hey, anything is better than the instant rubbish I have to contend with at the station. Thanks."

She watched Pauline expertly fill the coffee machine with water and measure out the coffee before placing all the relevant parts in the machine and flicking the switch. The coffee began to flow almost instantly into the carafe, and the wonderful aroma soon surrounded them. Pauline prepared two small cups and saucers and extracted a tub of cream from the integrated refrigerator. When the coffee machine spluttered to a halt, Pauline placed all the components on a tray and carried it over to the large leather corner unit in front of the bi-fold doors, which opened out onto the pristine, landscaped garden.

Pauline poured the coffee and placed the cup and saucer in front of Lorne. She sat back and expelled a weary sigh. "Right, now what is this about, Inspector?"

Lorne swallowed, took a sip of her steaming coffee then looked the woman in the eye. "I didn't want to tell you over the phone. It's with regret that I have to inform you that your husband is dead."

The woman frowned. "What? Are you sure?"

"Yes, his ID was still in his wallet when he was found."

Pauline placed her cup and saucer on the table and buried her head in her hands.

Lorne swiftly changed seats and sat alongside the distraught woman, hooking an arm around her shoulder. "I'm so sorry."

"How? Was it an accident?" Pauline reached for a tissue from the box on the coffee table and wiped her eyes.

"No. He was murdered. At this stage, we're unsure if he was in the wrong place at the wrong time or whether he was deliberately targeted."

"Where did this take place? I tried to call him last night and this morning, but the calls went direct to voicemail. I was concerned that he hadn't returned my calls, but he's super busy most of the time and rings me when he can."

"It was at the cinema in town. He was attacked from behind."

"How?" Pauline looked Lorne in the eye. "I need to know, Lorne."

"His throat was cut. I have to ask, did your husband have any enemies that we should know about?"

Pauline's eyes filled with fresh tears. "He was such a caring man. Yes, he'd had a few disagreements with work colleagues over the years, but he always sorted the problems out before they got out of hand."

"What was his job?"

"He worked in the city, stocks and shares."

"Was it a day off yesterday?"

"Yes, he told me that he was going to unwind for twenty-four hours while I was away. He loved horror films. I refused to go with him to see the ghastly things, so he went alone..."

"I'm so sorry. Would you mind giving me the address of where he worked? We'll have to interview his work colleagues ASAP."

Pauline's gaze drifted around the room and fell on a dresser along the far wall, next to the dining table. She rose unsteadily from the chair, but Lorne pulled her back down. "You sit there. I'll get it."

She retrieved a pad and pen then offered them to Pauline. With a shaking hand, the woman scribbled the name and address of the firm where her husband worked, tore off the sheet and gave it to Lorne.

"Do you need me to ring anyone to be with you?"

"No. I'd rather grieve for Gary on my own. Was there anything else?"

"Not at the moment. Can I get in touch if anything crops up in the next day or two?"

"Of course. Can I see him?"

Lorne nodded. "I can get the pathologist to ring you to arrange a time first thing in the morning."

"Thank you. I think it would help with the grieving process if I could say goodbye to him soon."

"I understand. I'll ring you tomorrow. Stay there. I'll see myself out."

Pauline nodded, a glimmer of an appreciative smile pulling her lips apart. "Goodbye, Inspector."

Lorne left the house, the heaviness in her legs matching what was going on in her heart as the woman's wailing followed her from the grand home. Choked with emotion on the drive home, she parked her car and walked through the back door and straight into Tony's arms.

"Hey, what's wrong? Not that I'm objecting."

"It's been a rough day. I just had to break the news to a lovely lady that her husband was murdered in a senseless attack. I love my job, but at times like this, I really do detest it, too."

He kissed the top of her head and squeezed her tighter. "That sucks. Sorry, love. Was the woman all right?"

"I think she's a tough lady. I hated leaving her with no one else around to support her. I hope I can find the bastard who has destroyed her life quickly."

"I'm sure you will. Do you have any idea who it might be?"

"We have the man on CCTV, but he was wearing a mask. I just hope this is a one-off incident and he doesn't try to repeat it."

"If there's anything I can do to help, let me know. I don't suppose you fancy much for tea then? What an awful birthday for you."

She pulled away and glanced up at him. "I'd totally forgotten all about that. Maybe I'll settle for an omelette today, and perhaps we can make up for it by going out for a meal at the weekend."

"Hey, it's your day. Whatever suits you, except... *you*'ll have to make the omelettes because I wouldn't have a clue where to start."

Lorne chuckled, relieving some of the tension that had been sitting on her shoulders since leaving the Ross's house. "How about I teach you?"

Tony pulled a face. "If you must."

They spent the next half an hour preparing all the ingredients for a Spanish omelette, and under Lorne's expert guidance, Tony created two fine-looking specimens, which they devoured over a much-needed bottle of wine.

CHAPTER THREE

Damn! Looks like this cinema doesn't use the fire exits to release the overflow. I'll have to go in the regular way now.

He waited until a crowd of people appeared, then he joined the queue. The woman in the kiosk was distracted by her manager, so she dealt with him swiftly, without looking up at him. He breathed a relieved sigh and followed the queue into the theatre and past the usherette. He would bide his time, sit in the middle of the last row and wait to see who sat close to him. A man picked a seat a few rows in front of him.

The lights dimmed and the adverts started to play. He paused before moving closer, making sure the man was alone. Then he bent down and, trying not to draw attention to himself, he switched rows to sit directly behind his target.

The voices filled his head. His breathing remained calm, but his heart rate had already begun to increase with the thought of what lay ahead of him. Waiting patiently, he played with the large knife sitting across his legs, its blade glinting as the scene on the screen changed during the commercials. As the last advert aired, a grin settled on his face beneath the convincing mask. The main event was due to start after a short interval, so he hid the knife in his jacket as the lights went on and the usherette circulated the theatre with her box of goodies. Once she'd passed his row, he returned the blade to his lap and patiently waited for the lights to dim and the loud introduction music to the movie to start.

Seconds later, the loud music erupted, silencing the audience, though he could still hear the occasional rustle of a sweets bag being opened. He would need to be patient for the part in the film he knew was the noisiest. It was mere seconds away. He gripped the knife in his right hand. The voices in his head began goading him, urging him to do it and berating him for not having the guts to go through with it. *I'll show them! I'm not a coward. I can do this. One slice, and it'll all be over. I can do this!*

A quick scan of the theatre showed him that everyone close to him was engrossed in the film. The time had come. He leaned forward and the blade glinted as if signalling for him to get on with it. He placed a hand over the man's mouth and slit his throat. No thrashing, no muffled cry, nothing. All was quiet. He sat there for another twenty minutes then casually left the theatre and strode into the foyer. The staff were all absent, no doubt on their coffee break while all the customers were otherwise engaged, giving him free rein to exit the cinema without getting into a conversation about why he didn't like the movie. He stepped outside and walked briskly to his car. He had a long journey ahead of him. He'd stayed up all night to hatch a plan that would keep the police on their toes for weeks and have them pulling their hair out.

CHAPTER FOUR

Lorne arrived at work in a determined mood. She said good morning to the desk sergeant as she breezed through the reception area, but something in his expression made her stop and speak to him. "Everything all right, Mick?"

His eyes rolled up to the tall ceiling. "I think there was another attack in the vein of what you're already investigating, ma'am."

"What? The cinema murder?"

"That's right."

"Why didn't I get the call?"

"One of the new lads was on duty last night. I've given him what-for and pointed out why you should have been called right away. It won't happen again."

"Let me have the details, Mick."

He handed her a sheet of paper. "Thanks, I better get to work on this immediately." She ran up the stairs and found Katy already sitting at her desk, nursing a cup of coffee. "Hi, Katy. Looks like we've got another one."

"Another what? Murder?"

"Yep, let me grab a coffee, and then we'll head over there."

"When did it happen?"

Lorne glanced down at the sheet at the same time as she inserted a fifty-pence coin in the vending machine. "Around ten thirty last night."

"Whoa! If it's the same killer, that's a bit brazen, even for their standards."

"That's what I thought. It has to be him, or her. It's too soon for a copycat killer to latch on to the details. Nothing has been aired on the news yet, not that I've seen anyway."

"The murder took place in the same location?"

"No. Different location, although the crime scene is another cinema. Maybe I should organise a press conference for this afternoon. It might prevent the culprit from striking again so soon."

"There again, he might up his game and revel in the euphoria of the TV exposure. Who knows with these mindless morons?"

Lorne walked into her office but called over her shoulder, "Will you ask Karen to call all the cinemas in the area, warn them to be vigilant in the meantime?"

"Sure. How long before we leave?"

"Give me five minutes." Lorne took a swig of coffee and picked up the phone. She dialled the pathology department at the nearby hospital. "Patti, I'm glad I caught you, it's Lorne."

"I was expecting your call. Another terrible murder on your patch. It has to be the same person, right?"

"I've just heard. Katy and I are on our way over there now. Is it the same MO?"

"Exactly the same. The victim was in his sixties, Harold Wise. Again, no sign of a struggle. He had no idea what was about to happen to him. Not sure I'll be able to go to the cinema again after dealing with these two victims."

"Damn. If you can give me his details, I'll visit his next of kin ASAP. By the way, the real reason I was ringing was because I dropped by to break the news to Gary Ross's wife last night, and she wants to know when she can see her husband. I said I'd call you first thing to make arrangements."

"This afternoon. I should be free around four to oversee the viewing."

"Thanks, Patti. I'm sure that will be okay. I'll ring her, and if there's a problem, I'll get back to you."

"No problem. I have to fly. I want to get this chap's PM out of the way."

"Thanks. Let me have the details via email as soon as you can." Lorne hung up and dialled Pauline's number on her mobile. "Hi, Pauline. How are you?"

"Hello, Lorne. I didn't sleep much, as you can imagine. Is it too early to ask if you've caught the culprit yet?"

"It is. I'm just on my way out to another crime scene. Looks like the offender has struck again."

Pauline gasped. "How dreadful. Not in the same place, surely?"

"No, a different cinema within the same vicinity. I've just rung the pathologist, and she said you're welcome to pop along there this afternoon around four. Can you make that?"

"Yes. I have no idea where to go, though."

Lorne gave her the address and told her in what area of the hospital she could find the mortuary. "I'll keep you informed during our investigation. I'm hoping to squeeze in a visit to your husband's place of work this afternoon. It depends how the day pans out with this new enquiry."

"I understand, although I'm sure you won't find anything untoward going on at Gary's firm."

"I have to agree it looks as though you're right, especially with this new incident happening within twenty-four hours of your husband's death."

~ ~ ~

Half an hour later, Lorne and Katy arrived at the second location. It had been years since Lorne had visited a cinema, but she'd had the misfortune of visiting two within the past two days, under gruesome circumstances. The staff were shell-shocked. By all accounts, the killer's second attack had been far more brazen and he'd struck during the main airing of the feature movie. The manager, Barbara Kinder, invited them into her office as soon as they arrived. She pulled hard on a cigarette. "Sorry, I need it to calm my nerves."

Lorne nodded. "Can you go through exactly what happened yesterday?"

"One of my guys was doing the rounds of the theatre, checking that everyone had departed for the evening and no one had left behind any stray items, the usual nightly procedure. Well, he approached the man, thinking that he'd dozed off during the film, and was horrified to find he'd been murdered."

"It must have come as a complete shock. Is that member of staff on duty today?"

"Yes. Dean is a very conscientious employee; it would take a lot for him to have a day off."

"We'll need to question him, if that's okay?"

"Of course. Want me to go and find him now? There's very little else I can tell you."

"Brilliant."

The manager left the office and returned accompanied by a bespectacled young man in his early twenties, with dark circles under his eyes. "Dean, these are Inspector Warner and Sergeant Foster. They'd like you to go over what you saw last night. I'll leave you to it." The manager left the room as Dean walked nervously round the desk and sat in his boss's chair.

"I didn't really see much, just the dead man with his throat cut. Scared the crap out of me, it did. I've never seen a dead body before. I haven't slept all night because all I could see were his bulbous eyes and that wound imprinted on my eyelids."

"It's okay. I'm sorry you had to experience such a dreadful ordeal. Time is a great healer, and the images fade, I promise you. Can you tell me if you noticed the man during the evening?"

His brow furrowed as he thought, then he shook his head. "I was on duty all night, but I don't recall him getting out of his seat to nip to the loo or anything."

"Was it very busy last night? Perhaps you remember the person who was sitting directly behind him?"

"I can't remember. I'd say if I did."

"Not to worry. Did anything out of the ordinary happen during the movie last night?"

Dean's brow wrinkled. "I don't understand. In what respect?"

"For instance, did the emergency door open during the evening?"

"Not that I can remember. Why?"

"I'm just trying to establish if the culprit escaped the theatre any other way. If no alarms went off—I take it the exits are alarmed—then the person who carried out this heinous crime must have left the building by the main exit."

"I suppose so. I have no idea. The manager can look through the CCTV footage, if that would help?"

"That would be a great help. I take it there was no reaction from the other customers to the man's death?"

"No, I think they must've thought he was sleeping, like I did. It was the pits discovering him in that state."

"I'm sure. If there's nothing else you can tell us, you're free to go, although we will need to take a statement from you over the next few days, while the events are still fresh in your mind. I'll get a uniformed officer to come and visit you here, if that's okay?"

"I'll let the manager know. I'm sorry I couldn't be much help."

"You did well. Try not to dwell on what you saw too much."

"I'll try," he said, vacating the chair and leaving the room.

The manager walked in a few moments later with a CD and placed it on the desk in front of Lorne. "I made you a copy of last night's CCTV footage. I know you didn't ask, but rather than twiddle my thumbs, I thought I'd do something useful."

"I appreciate that. Take a seat, Mrs. Kinder." The woman sat down before Lorne carried on. "This isn't public knowledge yet, but this is the second crime of this nature we're investigating within the last twenty-four hours."

The manager's eyes bulged. "You're kidding!"

"We should be having a press conference shortly. We believed the first attack was isolated, and perhaps personal, and didn't feel the need to share the news with other cinema houses. I assure you that has now been rectified. Had we known that we would be looking at a second incident, we would have warned other establishments to be vigilant."

"How dreadful. You just don't hear of this kind of thing going on in the UK, do you? What can I do to help prevent this happening again?"

"Honestly? I just think you need to be more attentive. We're dealing with a vile criminal who apparently is fond of wearing a disguise. That's all the facts we can divulge at present."

"I'll certainly tell my staff to be more alert, but would this person really walk into a cinema wearing a disguise? Maybe we should start searching people's bags as they enter?"

"It might be an idea."

In her peripheral vision, Lorne could see Katy shaking her head. "You'll be going against their human rights, I believe. I might be wrong, though."

"Hmm... Katy does have a point. We'll look into that and report back to you later today."

Lorne and Katy left the cinema feeling perplexed. "I hope we're not in for a spate of these crimes."

They climbed into the car before Katy replied, "Not telling you what you should do, but I think you should arrange a press conference ASAP rather than waiting for the afternoon news report. It could warn the public to be vigilant sooner, plus it might deter the culprit from taking another life."

Lorne tutted. "I agree. Let's head over to the victim's house before we go back to the station to get that organised. Oh… and, Katy, don't ever be afraid of voicing which avenue you think we should take during an investigation. We're partners, right? Shit-hot partners from what I can remember."

Katy chuckled. "Too right, we were. Might be a little while until I'm up to speed fully, but I'll keep tossing the ideas out there. If you're agreeable to them, then fine, but don't be afraid to slap my wrist if you see me overstepping the mark."

"Deal. However, you know I would never do that to a cop of your experience. So that's sorted."

~ ~ ~

In a sombre mood, Lorne rang the bell of the semi-detached house that had a pretty front garden full of colourful summer bedding plants, all laid out in straight rows. "Someone loved their garden. Let's hope it was Mrs. Wise and not her husband," Lorne stated quietly as they waited for the door to be answered.

"You're wasting your time there, loves. Mary has just nipped out with the dog. She'll be gone at least half an hour," an elderly gentleman shouted over the hedge.

"Ah, I see. Thanks for the warning. We'll wait in the car."

"Either that, or I could make you a brew. It's up to you." He shrugged and turned to go back into his house.

Lorne raised an eyebrow at Katy. "I'm easy. Feeling a little parched, as it happens."

"That's sorted then." They left Mrs. Wise's front garden and followed the elderly gent into his house.

"Make yourselves comfortable in the lounge. I'll be two ticks. Was it tea or coffee you wanted, ladies?"

"Coffee, both with milk and one sugar," Lorne called after him. "Thank you."

The man's lounge was a little too cluttered for Lorne's liking, but the room was cosy enough. She wandered over to the gold frame sitting on the mantelpiece and picked it up for a closer look. The photograph inside showed the man when he was about twenty to thirty years younger, standing with a beautiful redheaded lady.

Heroic Justice

"Ah, here we are then. That's my gorgeous wife, Delores." Carrying a tray of coffees, he nodded at the photograph. "Sadly, she passed away last year. Blasted cancer. It has affected every bloody family I know in the past decade. She did suffer come the end. She refused to have any further chemo, said her time had come and she'd accepted her fate. Glad she had because it was too traumatic for me to accept, although I did to keep the peace. She wouldn't have wanted to live a life of suffering for years on end. I've missed her every waking moment." His eyes misted up as he walked towards the coffee table and deposited the tray. "Listen to me rambling on. Loneliness is a bummer at times, ladies, I can tell you. Go on, help yourselves."

"You're very kind, sir. Sorry to hear about your wife. Were you married long?"

"Thirty-five years. Loved her from the second I laid eyes on her. Everyone loved Delores. Salt of the earth, she was. Would have given you her last penny if she thought you could do more with it than she could."

"She looked a gentle soul."

"She was. Anyway, enough about me, what are the police coming around looking for Mary for?"

Lorne smiled at the old man. "You're very astute, sir."

He waved his hand to interrupt her. "The name is Walter Enright. Be sure to put that down in your notebook now." He winked at Katy.

"Well, Mr. Enright, what can you tell us about the couple living next door?"

His brow crinkled, and his eyes narrowed. "I'm not daft. I might be old, but I ain't lost my marbles yet, miss."

"Meaning?"

"I know you wouldn't come knocking on Mary's door unless there was something important going on. Go on, you can tell me. I won't say a word, I promise. I'm the soul of discretion."

"We need to speak with Mary before we talk to anyone else regarding our visit, Mr. Enright. Have you known your neighbours long?"

"Twenty odd years. Harold and I are in the same bowling team together. Umm... that's crown green bowls, not ten-pin bowling." He laughed a little.

"Are you any good?" Lorne's heart went out to the man, who would soon learn that one of his best friends had departed this world.

45

"League champions last year. Not doing too good this year, though, mainly because the weather has been dire in the last few months. I prefer it when we play inside, less likely to be disrupted by what God sees fit to fling at us, if you know what I mean."

"I know, hope the season picks up for you. Does Harold have any other interests?"

"Let me think. Yes, for the life of me, I haven't a clue why, but he has a penchant for those damn horror films. Told me he was going to see one yesterday, actually had the cheek to invite me along. I declined, of course. Couldn't think of anything worse than sitting in a cinema, scared shitless for a couple of hours. Oops, I apologise for swearing."

"That's okay. Did he go to the cinema quite often?"

Mr. Enright's eyes narrowed, and he pointed at Lorne. "Has something happened to Harold? You spoke in the past tense there. Don't think I didn't pick up on that, miss."

Lorne sighed heavily and chewed her bottom lip. "Call it a slip of the tongue."

He shook his head vehemently. "I ain't stupid, and neither are you. Come to think of it, we usually go down the pub for a swift half in the evenings, but he neglected to show up down the social club last night. He ain't done nothing stupid, like imitating what he saw in that stupid film, has he?"

Lorne felt backed into the corner. She eyed Katy, who shrugged, indicating that she'd been rumbled. "The thing is, Mr. Enright—oh damn, I shouldn't tell you this until I've informed Mary..."

"He's either been banged up, or he's dead. Which is it?" he countered bluntly.

"As I've already stated, you're a very astute man. I'm sorry to have to inform you that it's the latter. Your friend was murdered during the movie he was watching."

The man left his seat and paced the room, his hand pulling through his thinning hair. "My God—*murdered*? I knew going to see one of those films would encourage someone to kill one day."

"We don't know that for certain, Mr. Enright. Please sit down."

"How can I?" he blasted, his voice becoming shaky. "He was my best pal. Poor Mary... she's going to be absolutely devastated by this news. I think I should be there when you tell her. She has a weak heart, and I'm afraid hearing this could kill her."

"Okay, I had no idea about her health issues. But you need to let us tell her, deal?"

"Of course." He walked over to the window and glanced down the road. "Bloody hell, she's on her way back now. I need to finish my cuppa first. Poor Mary," he repeated on the way back to his seat.

Lorne placed her hand over his, and felt it tremor beneath hers. "Please, try and calm down."

He snatched his hand away. "No need to tell me to calm down. I'm angry, yes, but I'm more upset for Mary than anything. They were a lovely couple. She doesn't deserve this. Bloody hell, Harold definitely didn't deserve to go out that way. I don't want to know the ins and outs of his death, but knowing that his life was ended in such a way is... well, frankly, deplorable."

"I know. Maybe it would be better if you left Katy and me to tell Mrs. Wise. I'm afraid you might not be a calming influence in your state."

"No, please. Okay, I'll take a few deep breaths, and I'll be right in a minute. I need to be there to comfort Mary. I'd never forgive myself otherwise."

"All right. Let's drink our coffees and then venture next door."

Katy moved over to the lace-covered curtains and nodded at Lorne, signifying that Mrs. Wise had arrived home. She returned to her cup and downed the remains of her coffee in one gulp.

"Okay, are we all ready?" Lorne patted Walter on the hand.

He smiled briefly at her and nodded.

The three of them stood up and left the house. As they entered Mrs. Wise's garden, she was just drying her dog's paws in the porch.

"Hello, Mrs. Wise," Lorne called out. "We're with the police. Is it all right if we speak with you for a moment?"

The woman looked up at all three of them in puzzlement. "Who the hell are you?" she demanded of Lorne. "Walter? What's going on?"

Lorne produced her ID before Walter had the chance to speak. "I'm DI Lorne Warner, and this is my partner, DS Katy Foster. Mind if we come in for a chat? It's important."

"Walter? You haven't answered my question. Oh my, this is about Harold, isn't it? He didn't come home last night." She turned to Walter. "I thought he was with you and still sleeping it off at your place. I thought I'd take Toby out for his walk and then come and give you two a telling off. It's not the first time he's been too drunk to come home. That's not it, though, is it? I can tell by your face that something is seriously wrong." Nerves made the woman chunter.

"Can we come in, please?" Lorne urged again.

"Go in there, Toby." Opening the door, she shooed the dog inside. "Be a good lad. Mummy will feed you in a moment." She led them down the hallway and into the front room. "Do I need to sit down for this?"

As Katy closed the front door, Walter swept past Lorne and took hold of Mary's arm, guiding her to the sofa. "It would be better, dear."

Lorne and Katy sat down in the easy chairs opposite the two dear friends. Lorne cleared her throat. "Mrs. Wise, it's with regret that I have to inform you of your husband's passing."

"Passing? I don't understand. Walter? What's she saying? That Harold is de..." Tears dripped onto her cheeks as she faced her companion for verification.

Walter nodded. "He's gone, love. It was a shock to me, too. I wanted to be here when the police officers informed you."

"Sorry, Mrs. Wise," Lorne jumped in quickly before Walter had a chance to tell her anything else. "It's not easy to say this, but your husband was the victim of a heinous crime when he attended the cinema yesterday."

Mrs. Wise's head swivelled between the three of them. "Are you saying he was murdered?" The woman's hand covered her chest, and her breathing faltered slightly.

"Where are your tablets, love? I'll get them for you."

Mrs. Wise pointed to the side cabinet alongside the far wall. "Quickly, please hurry."

Lorne dashed to sit by her side while Katy rushed out of the room to fetch a glass of water. Walter tipped a pill in the woman's outstretched hand, and Katy offered her the glass of water to wash it down.

The silence in the room drained Lorne. There was no easy way of telling a person that their significant other had died. It was even worse when the loved one had been murdered. She had no intention of going into detail about Mr. Wise's death—she decided the woman's heart wouldn't stand the news.

It was a good few minutes before Mrs. Wise had recovered enough to speak again. "He's really gone? I'll never see him again? I know we've had our ups and downs over the years, but he was my soulmate. I'm not sure I'll be able to go on now that he's gone."

Lorne gathered the woman's hand in her own. "Of course you can, Mrs. Wise. I know how shocking this seems right now..." She drifted off as the old woman began to sob. Lorne looked over at Katy for support, but her partner shook her head, not offering her any. Lorne then turned to Walter for assistance.

He placed his arm around Mrs. Wise's shaking shoulders and tried to calm her with soothing words. "Come now, Mary. I know Harold wouldn't want to hear you talking like this. You're a strong woman who has an abundance of friends willing to stand alongside you at times such as this. Try and be strong, love."

Mrs. Wise sniffled and wiped her nose and eyes on a hanky she pulled from her sleeve. "How will I cope, not having Harold around? I won't—I know I won't. He meant the world to me."

"You'll cope. I'm only next door, love. You know you only have to holler, and I'll be round in a jiffy."

Lorne sighed. "I'm sorry, please don't think I'm being insensitive, but I need to ask you if Harold had any enemies at all."

Mrs. Wise sharply turned to Lorne. "No, none who would *murder* him!"

"Could you tell me if Harold might have known a man named Gary Ross?" Lorne asked. "He worked in the city, with stocks and shares. Might Harold have had any dealing with him? With a retirement account, perhaps?"

"No, I don't think so... I don't know—" Mrs. Wise burst into sobs, which nearly took her breath away.

Harold shook his head. "Perhaps you two should go and start looking for the culprit. I can look after Mary now."

Lorne could see that her presence wasn't comforting the widow, who was too distraught to provide much information anyhow. And because she cared about people's feelings, unlike some of her colleagues, she thought it best that she and Katy take their leave. Lorne stood, and Katy followed her lead.

"Thank you so much for your time, Mrs. Wise. I'm so sorry to have brought you such terrible news. I'll leave my card. Please ring me at any time if you need my help—with anything. I hope to get back to you soon with some news."

"Thank you. Please do what you can to find this evil person," Mrs. Wise said, her hand shaking as she took the card. "He needs to be brought to justice."

"You have my guarantee that my team will do everything they can to solve this case."

After leaving the house, Lorne kicked out at a stone on the path.

"Now don't go blaming yourself, Lorne."

They jumped into the car, and Lorne rested her forehead on the steering wheel. "I have no idea why I feel so guilty right now, Katy, but I do. We have to catch this bastard before he strikes again."

Katy rubbed her arm. "We will. You're being too hard on yourself, as usual. Let's get back to the station and organise an appeal. At least it'll show the public that we're doing all we can to find the culprit."

"Are we, though, Katy? What are we doing, except visiting the victims' families to break the sad news? What evidence do we have? The culprit isn't daft. He was wearing a mask to put us off his scent. I'm at a loss where to go with the case now. Both attacks appear to be random, so how the hell do we track the person down when he could strike again at any location at any time?"

"Truthfully? It looks like our hands are tied, but we've been in this situation before, Lorne, and have always managed to overcome it."

Lorne sat upright and faced Katy. "Have we? I don't think we have, love. We've dealt with infuriating cases before, but at least we had some kind of lead to go on."

"You're being silly. Nine times out of ten, the leads on the other cases came in via a media appeal, which is next on our agenda. You're just feeling raw and inadequate because you couldn't help Mrs. Wise back there."

She smiled at her partner. "You're right. Okay, pep talk over. We're good, and on a roll again, I hope."

Lorne drove back to the station, where she gave Katy money to buy the coffees and spent the next few minutes on the phone arranging the appeal. Then she gathered the team and went over the information they had acquired so far, which was virtually zilch.

"Graham, I'd like you to concentrate on the CCTV footage around the alley and the nearby streets. Karen, can you search the archives for me, see if anything like this has ever been reported on our patch in the past? Maybe the culprit was put away a few years ago and has recently been let out of prison. I know it's a little farfetched, but at this time, we have very little else to go on. Katy, did you warn the other cinemas to remain vigilant?"

"Yep, I've already done that."

Heroic Justice

"So, for now we'll follow up on leads from other cases, and I'll crack on with my paperwork until I have to face the cameras in a few hours. Do your best, peeps. As it stands, I think this guy is going to get away with more than the two murders he's already committed."

CHAPTER FIVE

His stomach muscles constricted. The thrill running through him felt different. This one was definitely going to be a challenge. He'd never frequented this cinema before, and he had no idea what the film was about or how to time his kill. He sat there, listening and watching the movie. It began as a fairly quiet film, more of a psychological thriller than the horror films he'd used to cover his previous crimes. He needed to be far more patient preparing his next move. The cinema was slightly smaller than the others and had fewer seats, which meant the risks were higher. He was amazed how many people attended the matinee viewings of such films.

One man in particular drew his interest. He was alone and engrossed in the movie. He left his seat and sat behind his chosen victim. His knife at the ready, he waited for the right moment to present itself. As the drama unfolded on the screen, the tempo of the soundtrack increased, and he sensed the time was near. That's when the voices started. *Coward! You haven't got the guts to do it! Go on, what are you waiting for? Do it, do it, do it...*

Shut up. I'll show you how much courage I have. Leaning forward, he quickly drew the knife across the man's throat. At first, the man's hands clutched at his neck, but that proved pointless and his head dropped forward onto his chest.

He waited another five minutes before leaving the cinema and exiting through the foyer. As he stepped out onto the street, his heart raced at the speed of a Formula One car taking to the track at Silverston.

I did it... number three under my belt. Let's see what the coppers think of that now.

CHAPTER SIX

Nearly a week passed before the team received a response from the public appeal. Not a single call had come their way, but the appeal appeared to have worked on the killer, as no further victims turned up.

When Lorne arrived at the station first thing on Wednesday, Karen pointed out an alert that had popped up on her computer.

"In Manchester?"

Karen nodded. "I created an alert, thinking the culprit might move to a neighbouring county. I never dreamed he'd travel all the way up there. It has to be the same guy, boss. It's definitely the same MO, anyway."

"Find out who's dealing with the case in Manchester and get them on the phone for me. I'll be in my office, downing two cups of coffee before I speak to them." As usual, Lorne paused just inside the doorway to her office. There was no smell of Pete to comfort her, though.

The phone on her desk rang as she settled into her chair. "Hi, Karen."

"Boss, I have DI Hero Nelson on the phone for you."

"Is this some kind of windup? Who the heck calls their child Hero?" Lorne asked in disbelief as she took a sip from one of the coffee cups in front of her.

Karen chortled. "Someone with a sense of humour, a warped one at that. Anyway, I'll put him through."

"You're probably right about that. Thanks, Karen."

"Hello, this is DI Nelson, Inspector, can I help?"

"I hope so, DI Nelson. I hear you've had a murder occur on your patch in the last twenty-four hours."

"No doubt we've had a few, Inspector. This is Manchester, after all. Is there one case in particular that you're interested in?"

"The one that took place in the cinema."

"Ah yes, appalling case. Totally overkill in my book. There's no way the victim could have survived such brutality."

"Well, the thing is, we had two such cases happen in our neck of the woods only last week."

"Get away with you. Seriously?"

"Deadly serious. I put an appeal out in the media this time last week, and we haven't had another incident occur since then. Looks like the killer went to ground and resurfaced up there perhaps."

"I can see your logic, Inspector. But there's also an alternative that we should consider here—"

"A copycat killing? Yes, I'd already thought of that. However, my gut feeling is denying that. Sorry, I tend to listen to my gut, and it's rarely wrong."

DI Nelson laughed. "A girl after my own heart. I'm very much the same, Inspector. So, what do you think we should do about this? Do you think the culprit is likely to strike again?"

"He's struck twice on consecutive days down here. My team rang all the cinemas in the area to warn them to be more vigilant, but it proved to be a useless exercise because he managed to kill a second victim. Do you have CCTV footage of the killer?"

"Yes, not a very good position, though."

"Could you make out if he was wearing a disguise?"

"Let me get the clip up on my screen, just a second. Ah, here it is. No, I have a slight side shot of his face but can't make out any distinguishing features."

"Damn, even so, I really do think the cases are connected. Maybe we can get both shots analysed for similarities in height and weight?"

"Good idea. So, how do you think we should proceed? I'm all ears."

Lorne chewed her lip as she thought. "I'm open to suggestions. It wouldn't be the first time I've dealt with a joint case. I had to travel to Norfolk a few years ago to take down a vile matriarch who carried out a crime on my patch. Luckily the inspector in charge of the case up there welcomed my involvement as we went on a course at Hendon together."

"Well, I've heard a lot about the infamous Lorne Simpkins-Warner and how she always gets her man. It would be an honour for me to work alongside you, if that's the route we need to take to capture this criminal."

Heroic Justice

Lorne felt the colour rise in her cheeks. "I'm glad we're not in the same room as you'd witness me blushing right now. I'm at a disadvantage in that I've never heard your name mentioned before. I'm sure it would have remained lodged in my mind if I had."

"Ah, you're referring to the Hero part. The truth is, I hate using it. Most people call me Nelson or the odd few call me Patch, if that helps."

"Patch it is then. Will we have to run things past our DCIs first? Mine's okay most of the time, though he does blow hot and cold sometimes."

"Maybe they come from a special mould because that's exactly how I would describe mine. His mood changes with the breeze. Kind of old-school type of DCI. I suppose we'd better run it past them, but yes, if they agree, then I think we should put our heads together and join forces on this one."

"Brilliant. I look forward to working with you. I think it would be better if my partner and I travel to Manchester as the culprit seems to be striking there at present."

"I'll have a word with my DCI and get back to you within a few hours. How's that?"

Lorne smiled. She liked this man. He seemed really friendly compared to some of the DIs she'd had to deal with over the phone in the past. Maybe he was an arsehole in real life, but only time would tell on that one. "I'll go and see my DCI now, too. Speak soon, Patch. Oh, can you email me the CCTV footage you have?"

"Give me your address, and I'll do it now."

After giving him her email details, she hung up then drank her two cups of coffee. When she opened the email that had just pinged in her inbox, she was certain the man was the same suspect.

She popped down the corridor to DCI Roberts's office, where his PA, Trisha, greeted her warmly.

"Is he free?"

Trisha nodded. "He is. Just knock and go in. He'll want to see you, Inspector."

Lorne rolled her eyes up to the ceiling. "I'm not so sure after what I have to share with him."

Trisha held her hand up in the air and crossed her fingers. "I'll cross my toes and eyes, as well, if you think that will help."

"Thanks, anything and everything is greatly received." She rapped on the door then waited for Sean Roberts to beckon her.

"Come in." His tone was flat, and she had trouble deciphering what type of mood he was in.

She entered the room and closed the door behind her. "Do you have a spare five minutes, sir?"

"I have. Take a seat, Lorne. What's wrong?"

She exhaled a heavy breath. "I might need to go to Manchester."

"Well, that got my attention. May I ask why?"

"It's work related, don't worry. The killer we're after seems to have taken up his activities there."

"How do you know it's the same killer?"

"Apart from the same MO, the DI investigating the murder sent me a clip of the CCTV footage. It certainly looks like the same person, even from the brief snippet I saw of him. My gut is telling me that it is, too." She added the last part and dipped her head onto her chest.

"Ah, the infamous Warner gut instinct at play yet again. Okay, I'm willing to play along with that. You've spoken to the DI in charge of the case, I take it? And he's agreeable to you going up there to interfere on his turf?"

"Why do you have to say it like that, Sean? I get bloody results, don't I? What does it matter in what part of the country that takes place? You can be such a..." They were old friends, more than that, and sometimes she found it hard thinking of him as her superior, especially when he challenged her.

"Stop biting, Inspector. You should know damn well when I'm winding you up by now."

"Sorry."

"You're not, and you know it. Who else will be going with you? Katy?"

"I haven't cleared it with her yet. Would you object to that?"

"Well, I'd rather have one of you remain behind. She would be the ideal candidate, considering she used to be in your job. Can't you take another member of the team with you?"

Lorne fell quiet for a moment as she thought over her options. "Actually, they'll be of more use here. I'll go by myself, if that's allowed?"

He lowered his voice. "I haven't said this, but why don't you take Tony on the trip with you?"

The cogs started turning in her head. It had been a while since they'd been away together. Charlie still had a few weeks before she

Heroic Justice

enrolled at the police training college, so she and Carol could look after things at the rescue centre.

"Well?" Roberts prompted impatiently, his expression blank, hard to read.

"I'm planning things out in my mind. I'll have to run it past Katy first. She's only just come back off maternity leave. I'm not sure she'd relish taking on the challenge of filling my shoes just yet."

"She will. I'll be here to lend her a helping hand. Let's face it: you'll be the one up there in the firing line as it were. Katy will just be handling the day-to-day running of the team back here."

"I'll still need to ask her. I'm not in the habit of presuming anything, Sean. You know that."

"Yeah, I seem to recall." He grinned, a glint in his eye.

She fidgeted uncomfortably in her seat. "Okay, so, you're giving me the go-ahead as long as I get things covered around here?"

"That's what I said, yes. Now if you'll excuse me, I have a few calls to make." He reached for the telephone, dismissing her.

"Thanks, Sean. You won't regret this."

As she reached the door, he called out her name.

"Lorne, I better not. Oh, by the way, I received a list of the new recruits who are set to join the training course, and one name in particular stood out."

"Yeah, she advised me about that last week—*after* she'd been accepted. I had no idea she wanted to join the police. It's put us in a dilemma back at the ranch. I'm in line for a kennel manager if you know of any suitable candidates."

"I bet. I'll keep my ears open. Tell Charlie I sent my congratulations, will you? Umm... dare I ask what Tom has said about her decision?"

"I had a conversation with him about it last week. He was angry at first, until his new wife calmed him down and made him see sense. Charlie's a young woman now, and she isn't as daft as he thinks she is. He still regards her as his little girl. Most fathers do, right?"

"I suppose. Okay, slap her on the back for me anyway."

"Thanks, Sean. I'll get back to you when I firm up my plans about Manchester. Would it be all right if I put my hotel on expenses?"

"Why not? Enjoy your time away with Tony, if he agrees to go with you."

"I appreciate that, thanks."

CHAPTER SEVEN

Hero hung up and sat back in his chair at the same time his partner, Julie Shaw, entered the room. "Everything all right, sir?"

"To be honest with you, Julie, I'm not sure."

Her brow wrinkled in puzzlement. "Meaning what, exactly, sir?"

"Meaning that this case we're working has been highlighted by another force, and the lead investigator is on her way to see us."

"How strange. Has that ever happened before, sir?"

"Not in person. I've had inspectors from other forces ring me up, but I don't recall anyone ever turning up on my doorstep to lend a hand. But then, I hear this woman likes to do things differently. She has a reputation for not letting anything get in the way of making an arrest."

Julie sighed and rolled her eyes. "Sounds challenging. Does that mean she'll be running the show when she gets here?"

"I wouldn't say it quite like that, but I think she'll expect to be listened to when she speaks. We'll have to see what happens when she arrives. She's on her way now. I don't want to pass any judgement on her either way at this stage. Let's hold back our thoughts until we see what she's made of, eh? Like I said, her reputation precedes her."

"What's her name?"

"DI Lorne Warner. I seem to recall she had dealings with one of the UK's most corruptible villains a few years ago under her old name, just in case you're thinking about looking her up," Hero said, reading his partner's obvious intentions.

"I'll see what I can dig up. I take it the case is on hold until her arrival."

"No, far from it. I'll be dropping by the mortuary this morning to see how the PM went." He fell silent, and it didn't go unnoticed by Julie.

Heroic Justice

"Want me to do that side of things on this one, boss, in the circumstances?"

He looked her in the eye through a mist of tears. "I've got to tackle going there eventually; I might as well do it at the first opportunity."

Julie rose from her seat and walked towards the door. "My offer still stands. I know how raw you must be feeling inside."

"Thanks. I'll be fine." He watched his partner leave the room and walked over to the window. He lifted the catch to open it a little, finding the room closing in on him all of a sudden. The past week or so had been a nightmare for him and his family. His mother was recuperating at his house after the accident that had taken his father's life. The funeral the previous week had devastated his entire family. Louie, who was older than the twins, understood what was going on more than his siblings did, but it hadn't stopped him breaking down in tears every now and again. That set the twins off, although he suspected Zoe and Zara cried mainly because they saw their older brother upset. Sometimes, it felt like a never-ending cycle.

His mother was putting on a brave face and disguising her emotions well in front of the children during the day, but when the kids went to bed, she broke down. Seeing that, tore Hero's heart in two. He was busy consoling every member of his family while suppressing his own grief. His wife, Fay, had given him the space he needed and cuddled him in bed at night when he finally let loose all the pent-up emotions that burden anyone who's lost a parent. But it was how his twin sister, Cara, was dealing with the loss that perturbed him the most. She had distanced herself from everyone, told them that she needed to grieve for her father in her own way, by being by herself. She hadn't had the courage to return to work. Her commanding officer had so far been extremely understanding, but only yesterday, he'd collared Hero in the corridor, wanting to know when he could expect Cara to return to duty. He had to be honest with him and say he didn't have a clue as she didn't appear to be coping very well.

Hero tried calling her every day, but her mobile always went into voicemail until the evening, and when she answered, her side of the conversation consisted of only one-word responses. If Lorne Warner weren't descending on his doorstep in a few hours, he would have called around to see Cara that evening, suffering her wrath of slamming the door in his face if necessary. He missed her. The kids, his mum and Fay missed her, too. Shutting herself away wasn't about to ease her grief anytime soon.

He closed his eyes, and his father's smiling face filled his mind. *I miss you, old man. If you could wave a healing wand over everyone and urge them to get on with their lives, I'd really appreciate it.*

The phone on his desk rang, interrupting his thoughts. He picked it up and listened to the chatty pathologist, Susan Rendell. It certainly put life back on track for him.

"Whoa, slow down, Susan. You're going faster than an express train."

"I know, sorry. I have a lot ahead of me today."

"Why don't you save what you have for me, and I'll drop over and see you. I was just about to do that anyway."

"Are you sure? It's not too soon for you?"

"No. I appreciate everyone trying to wrap me up in cotton wool, but I'm fine. The sooner I get back to normal, the better. See you in ten minutes."

After hanging up, he unhooked his jacket from the back of the chair and marched through the incident room. Julie's interest was being held by what was on her computer screen. Hero leaned over her shoulder and whistled. "Wow, is that her?"

"Yep. Lorne Warner, formerly known as Simpkins. No wonder she went after that Unicorn guy. He was holding her daughter hostage and using her as a prostitute in a human-trafficking ring."

"Shit, really?"

"Here's the crunch. Her daughter was only fourteen at the time."

Hero let out a long, low whistle. "Christ. I hope she strung the bastard up by his knackers."

"She did more than that. She retired from the force and set off to France to get her retribution with a couple of MI6 officers. Apparently, she later married one of them. Let's just say, we can't go wrong having her on our side in this case, boss. The crux will be how much control she'll want during the investigation."

Hero straightened up. "Well, we'll have to wait and see on that one. I'm not averse to having someone of her capabilities around us. The more, the merrier if it means we get this moron off the streets quicker. I'll be back soon. I have a date with a talkative pathologist to attend."

"Good luck."

Heroic Justice

The mortuary corridor felt more unwelcoming than usual, and he couldn't prevent the shudder rippling down his spine as he made his way towards Susan's office.

She looked up and welcomed him with a smile. "Come in, Hero. Can I get you a coffee?"

"Thanks, that'd be great."

Susan poured two cups of coffee from the filter machine behind her and handed one to Hero before sitting down. "Cheers, how are you coping? I bet it was hard coming here today."

"It was, but needs must. I'm doing as well as can be expected. Trying to hold it together while those around me are falling apart with grief. Dad was such a special man. Everyone loved him. We were surprised by how many showed up at his funeral last week. That really brought it home to us just how many lives he touched with his quirky sense of humour and caring manner. We'll miss the old sod."

"Dare I ask how your mum is?"

"She has good days and bad. Her recuperation from the operation is going slower than anticipated, but the doctor said that in the circumstances, that's to be expected. It's slow, but she's improving—that's the main thing. It's my sister that is really concerning me. She's cut herself off from the family."

Susan placed a hand over his. "Give her time. Grief affects people in different ways, love. She'll come through it in the end. Don't give up on her."

"Thanks. I've no intention of doing that, but I need to hold her in my arms, need her to reassure me just as much as I need to reassure her that everything is going to be okay. Twins have a bond that other brothers and sisters just don't have. That's the hard part in all this. We should be supporting each other, but she's made it perfectly clear that she intends to keep the whole family at arm's length."

"Stay strong and just be there when she needs you."

"I will. Enough of my problems. What news do you have to share about the PM? Then I'll fill you in with what other devastating news is about to descend on me."

Susan tilted her head. "Something bad?"

"You first."

She shook her head and pulled a file from the pile on her desk. "Well, I'm not saying I have anything truly newsworthy to tell you, but I do think this person, in my opinion, has killed before."

"Now you've got my interest. What makes you think that?"

"The ease at which the knife was used. It was one straight cut. Usually, a first-timer would hesitate halfway through, as if debating with themselves if they should proceed or not."

"Well then, I've not heard that before, but I can definitely understand the logic. It also leads me on to my news. I have an inspector on her way up from London, who will be working alongside me on this one."

"Can I ask why?" Susan asked before taking a sip of her coffee.

"Two crimes similar to this have taken place in the last week in her area. We think we're looking at the same killer and he's possibly moved locations. Why? We've yet to find that out."

"Wow, okay. I'll need to confer with the pathologist who is dealing with the other two corpses in that case. The more people's brain power we can use, the quicker we're likely to apprehend the culprit."

"I can get that information to you later when she arrives."

"How do you feel about a joint investigation?"

Hero shrugged. "Never had to deal with one before, Susan. Ask me that question again in a few days or weeks."

She laughed. "Hang in there. In my experience, female inspectors tend to go the extra mile, mainly because of the pressure they're under from their superiors, performing in a bloody man's world."

Tutting, he shook his head. "That's crap. No one thinks like that nowadays, do they?" he asked, uncertainty filling his mind once he'd said it out loud.

"I'm telling you, it's true. Some women inspectors can be right bitches in the process, though—something for you to be wary of." His eyes bulged, making Susan roar with laughter. "Get away with you, I'm sure you'll cope. You always do."

"We'll see. If I wasn't apprehensive about this inspector descending upon us before, I bloody am now."

CHAPTER EIGHT

Just after lunch, Lorne and Tony arrived at the Manchester police station. At first glance, it appeared to be just as run down as Lorne's back in London, despite the renovations her station had gone through over the previous few years.

"Are you ready for this?" Lorne asked Tony as trepidation made her stomach do several somersaults.

"I am. The question is, are you? This isn't like you, Lorne. You look petrified. Why the apprehension? I thought you said he sounded okay on the phone."

"He did. It's just me being silly. Come on, let's not dillydally out here. Let's dive into the unknown." Ever the gentleman, Tony opened the large front door for Lorne to enter first.

She produced her warrant card for the desk sergeant. "Hi, I'm Detective Inspector Lorne Warner, and this is my husband, Tony. DI Nelson is expecting us."

The sergeant smiled and nodded. "I'll just give him a buzz, ma'am."

"Thanks."

Lorne and Tony stepped aside as the man placed the call.

"He'll be right down, Inspector."

Lorne nodded and let out a large breath.

"What is wrong with you? I've never seen you like this before," Tony said.

"You know me—I hate stepping into the unknown. I'm out of my comfort zone here, Tony. Give me some slack."

He placed an arm around her waist and squeezed her. "I'm here to protect you. Never fear, little lady."

She laughed and dug him in the ribs just as a tall, slim, well-dressed, handsome man walked into the room.

"Hi, I'm DI Nelson. You must be Lorne Warner."

"I am. Sorry about that. This is my husband, Tony Warner."

DI Nelson's brow furrowed as he shook hands with Tony. "Pleased to meet you. I was under the impression that you would be coming alone, Inspector."

"Maybe we could go to your office, where I can fully explain why Tony is here."

"Of course, this way."

Lorne turned to Tony and rolled her eyes. "He didn't look too impressed about you being here."

Tony winked. "Leave him to me. He'll come around."

They followed DI Nelson up the stairs and into his office. Lorne felt his team's eyes on her as she passed. She kept her gaze trained on Nelson's back instead of acknowledging the team one by one.

"Can I get you a drink?" DI Nelson offered as if just remembering his manners.

"Two coffees, white with one sugar, thanks. It's been a long trip," Lorne replied, smiling.

As Lorne and Tony sat, DI Nelson poked his head into the outer office and ordered the coffee. DI Nelson settled into his chair, and after a few moments, a woman wearing a scowl appeared with the drinks and deposited them on the desk in front of Lorne and Tony.

Lorne smiled at the woman. "Thank you. It's much appreciated."

"Sorry, I should introduce you. This is my long-suffering partner, DS Julie Shaw, although I think she'll be joining the rank of inspector soon enough."

Lorne locked gazes with Shaw. "Pleased to meet you, and good luck with your foreseeable promotion."

"Thanks. I'm going to need it," the sergeant replied sharply.

"Not wishing to step on your toes, Inspector, but maybe your partner should be involved in the meeting we're about to have. It would save you having to repeat what we have to say anyway."

"Julie?" Nelson tilted his head, awaiting his partner's response.

She shrugged. "Why not? I'll go and get another chair."

Julie collected the chair, first bashing it against the doorframe then Tony's chair as she tried to squeeze past in the confined space, to sit alongside DI Nelson.

"Okay, my first question is, why is your husband here? It's not usual police procedure for spouses to accompany inspectors on investigations, is it?" Nelson asked.

"I know, and ordinarily, I would agree with you. Actually, it was my DCI's idea. Tony used to be an MI6 agent. He assisted me—

more than assisted me, to be fair—when I captured a criminal a few years ago. We've been together ever since. He's also a private investigator."

"I see. Yes, I remember the case well. The Unicorn, wasn't it? Nasty piece of goods he was by all accounts. Didn't you have to leave the force in order to track the bastard down, Inspector?"

Lorne chuckled. "You have done your homework well. Yes, I had just begun renovating houses when Tony got wind of where the Unicorn had resurfaced. At first, when he came knocking on my door, I was reluctant to get involved in the investigation, but... well, after what that bastard did to my daughter, my protective mothering instincts got the better of me. I couldn't stand for another young woman to go through what my Charlie did, so we set off for France. The rest is history, and Tony and I have been inseparable since then. I swear, that's the end of me being gushy." She laughed, and so did the others.

"Then I guess that's settled. All right with you, Julie?"

The sergeant shrugged, and her lips parted in a slight smile. "I suppose so."

Nelson banged his hand on the desk. "Well, that's sorted then. Welcome aboard, Mr. and Mrs. Warner. Let's hope we catch this deviant as soon as is humanly possible. Three deaths puts him right up there in the serial killer bracket."

"That's why we're here. It's not often that I chase around the country looking for a killer. He's a particularly nasty individual. Some might even put him in the cowardly category because of the way he kills his victims—from behind, without giving them the chance to defend themselves. We have to figure out why he's targeting people watching movies. Why not choose his victims on the streets? There really are too many unanswered questions on this one, and I don't mind admitting that I'm finding it more than just a tad frustrating."

Nelson nodded, and Julie cleared her throat.

"Go ahead, Julie," Hero said.

"I was just going to say that if we're going to discuss the case, wouldn't it be better to do that in the incident room, in front of the rest of the team?"

Lorne smiled and nodded at the sergeant. "I'm not averse to that. It's the way I always work with my team."

"Okay, we'll do that. Shaw, why don't you go and get things organised, while we finish our drinks and get more acquainted with each other?"

The sergeant left her chair and returned to the incident room. As soon as the door closed behind her, Nelson let out a relieved sigh.

Lorne wasn't about to let that pass. "Everything all right between you two?"

Nelson laughed. "That bloody obvious, eh?"

"Somewhat. Is it because she's doing her inspector's exam?"

Nelson shook his head. "No. I'm genuinely pleased for her, otherwise I wouldn't have put her name forward. Let's just say we merely tolerate each other at times. However, we do make a cracking team. Half the time, she spends scowling at me—that is, when she's not tampering with that confounded phone of hers, which drives me to distraction. I'm sure she does it just to jangle my nerves."

"She seems nice enough. A little surly, but nice all the same."

"Enough about her. I want to know more about the PI business, Tony. Lucrative, is it?"

Tony glanced sideways at Lorne and sniggered. "Not really. It keeps me out of mischief, though. Lorne set the agency up in between her terms in the Met. We started getting a few customers, so Lorne thought it would be a good idea if I continued the business after she returned to the force. I run it with my partner, Joseph. We make a pretty good team. Only covered a few minor cases, nothing too taxing, up until now."

"Slap me down if you think I'm being nosey, but can I ask why you left MI6? It must have been hard going back to a 'normal job' after being a top government agent?"

"I'd still be working for them if it wasn't for the Taliban."

"Oh, I'm confused. What have the Taliban got to do with anything?"

Tony swung his false leg up onto the desk. "The bastards cut off my leg on my last deployment."

The colour drained from Nelson's face. "Jesus Christ. I had no idea. Sorry, mate. They're bloody animals, that lot."

"I agree. I'm fine about it. We cope all right with me having a bum leg, don't we, Lorne?"

"We do. Mind you, it gets a little dodgy around the rescue centre now and again when Tony gets stuck in the mud."

Heroic Justice

"Rescue centre? You're not telling me you run one of those in your spare time, as well?"

"Afraid so. Another one of my bright ideas that I've palmed off onto another member of my family. I hate to see any form of cruelty, to dogs especially. Most of our dogs are full-time borders. It's not ideal for them to be living in the kennels all the time, but what's the alternative? Living the rest of their lives either being abused by their hateful owners or scavenging for food like lost souls on the street? Sorry, I need to rein myself in a little. I'm passionate about animal welfare and speaking up for the dogs who have no voices."

"I have a Rottweiler cross called Sammy. I totally get where you're coming from. He's an absolute treasure and regarded as an important part of our family. The kids love him, especially the twins."

"Twins? How many kids do you have?"

"Three. The oldest boy is from my wife's previous marriage, but her ex isn't around, and I'm thankful for that. Louie's a wonderful child. I regard him as my own, and he absolutely adores his twin sisters. We're lucky that they all get on really well. Dread to think what life would be like if they spent all their time screaming at each other."

"Not sure I could cope with three kids. One was enough for me."

"Charlene, right?"

Lorne pointed at him and winked. "You seriously have done your homework on me."

"I like to know who I'm working with. I promise I didn't dig too deeply. I saw enough to know that I think we would get along—that's the main thing."

"It is. I think we're going to get along just fine. Charlie informed us last week that she's just enrolled at Hendon."

"Wow, how do you feel about that?"

"I was gobsmacked at first. She's an intelligent girl and has been through such a lot—too much—in her young life that I think she'll breeze through the training and make a stonkingly good police officer."

"With your guidance, she can't go wrong. My twin sister, Cara, also joined the force a few years ago. She's been through a tough time in the last six months, so she's not in a good place right now."

"May I ask why?"

"First of all, her boyfriend, also a copper, was killed in the line of duty. This guy cried wolf, and when Cara's fella turned up with

67

his partner, they were ambushed. Didn't stand a chance. And recently, our parents were involved in a car accident. Mum's still recuperating, but we lost our father in the end. My sister is struggling to come to terms with losing Dad."

"And how are you coping, Hero?" Lorne asked, presuming that no one had asked him. There was an unspoken code that said men had to put on a brave face.

Nelson's eyes bulged. "Nice of you to ask. I'm getting there. I miss the old bugger, but I wouldn't want to see him struggling and having to survive in a wheelchair. He couldn't have handled that. Anyway, less of all this maudlin talk. We should drink up and address the team. Not that we have much to go on."

"I know. Something will break soon. We had to come up here, strike while the iron is hot and all that. Have you had any reaction from the TV appeal that you put out? Oops, ignore me. I'm sure you'll fill us in out there."

"I can see similarities in us, Inspector. Please, once we've addressed the team, don't feel as though you need to hold back. Our priority has to be to rid the streets of this madman and quickly. I won't have egos getting in the way of this investigation."

"I agree. There will be times I might race ahead, but feel free to rein me in."

"Good luck with that one, because I always fail miserably," Tony joked, earning himself a slap on the arm.

They finished their coffee and stepped into the incident room, where the team eagerly awaited them. Over the next hour, Lorne and Nelson went through every aspect of the case and how they planned to go forward. The first order of business was to contact the cinemas in the area and warn them to be on the lookout for a masked man. Hero put a member of his team on the task right away.

By late afternoon, they had exhausted all the clues and worked out how they were going to proceed. Feeling drained, Lorne asked DI Nelson if she and Tony could be excused for the rest of the day to sort out a hotel for their stay.

They located a reasonably priced hotel in the heart of the city. Though nothing special, it was adequate for their needs. Lorne didn't intend on them spending much time in the room anyway. Today was an exception—travelling always took its toll on her.

Lorne and Tony had a quick shower and changed before heading down to the hotel's restaurant. The waitress promptly appeared at their table to take their orders. The salmon en croute caught their eye and Tony ordered a bottle of Chablis to accompany the meal. The restaurant had a lovely intimate feel to it, dimly lit, all decked out in burgundy and pink.

"It's been ages since we went out for a meal together. Why is that?"

"Maybe because you have a penchant for takeaways," Tony jested.

"I do *not*. They're just convenient after a hard day's graft. Seriously, we should do this more often. It's making me all warm and fuzzy inside."

One of Tony's eyebrows rose up into his hairline. "Oh, is that right, Mrs. Warner?"

Lorne reached across the table for his hand. "Wouldn't it be nice to spend more time together, without all the stresses of work hanging over our heads?"

"Of course it would. What are you saying, Lorne? That you want to ditch the rescue centre?"

Lorne gasped. "No, I could never do that. I was just thinking how wonderful it would be spending more time together in the evenings. We have the ideal opportunity with Charlie going off to the police training college over the next few months."

"Ah, but you're forgetting one thing: that will also mean our workload back at the kennels is going to increase during that time."

Lorne shrugged. "I know. No harm in dreaming a little now and again. We need to sort out a replacement sharpish. That's nigh impossible to do when we're a couple of hundred miles away from home, though."

"Carol said she'd do extra hours when needed until the right applicant came along, so there really isn't any need to concern yourself about that side of things. It may prove to be a distraction too many in solving this case."

"You always talk a lot of sense. Okay, any kennel problems are firmly pushed to the back of my mind for now. What do you make of DI Nelson?"

"He seems a decent enough chap. I'm not privy to his arrest record, but his team seem to respect him. Not sure the same can be said about his sergeant. Julie Shaw, was it?"

"Yeah, the jury is definitely still out for me on that one. I caught her looking at me a few times when I was addressing the team, and it sent a chill shooting up my spine. Maybe she's the type that rubs her hands when certain colleagues screw up. I don't know. I might be doing her an injustice. I barely know the woman."

Tony laughed. "Well, I certainly didn't get that impression. Do you really think if she was that bad her name would have been put forward for inspector?"

"I suppose not, but there's something off about her, Tony. Take my word on that."

"Oh yes, the famous Lorne Warner gut instinct strikes again."

"Mock me at your peril, Agent Boy. We'll see how things progress, shall we?"

The waitress appeared and placed their meals in front of them. *Salmon en croute, new potatoes, broccoli, and mangetout. Who could ask for more?* "It looks delicious, thank you."

"Can I get you any accompaniments?" the waitress asked with a broad smile.

"Some tartare sauce would be nice," Lorne replied for both of them.

They devoured the meal, hungrier than they'd first realised, but decided to forgo a dessert. Then they went back to their room, feeling slightly tipsy after consuming a second bottle of wine between them. It had been good to let their hair down for a change. Lorne just hoped it didn't interfere with work the following morning.

Lorne snuggled up to Tony, and they both drifted off to sleep before either one had the chance to bid the other goodnight.

CHAPTER NINE

Peering around a building close to the cinema, he watched a large group of people run up the steps and into the foyer to get out of the downpour. His heart raced in anticipation. He was already soaked to the skin, increasing his anger and determination to punish someone before the night was over. Switching from the afternoon matinees, where the kill was easy, meant that all his senses were heightened. He could smell the fear in his victims before the knife sliced their flesh, or was that his imagination? His hearing picked up the gaining momentum in their breath as they felt his presence behind them, or so he assumed.

The crowd whisked through the foyer, then it was his turn to pay for his seat.

"Just the one ticket?" the girl sitting in the kiosk asked, not even bothering to make eye contact.

"Yeah, just one." He purposefully kept his tone light and breezy, to discourage her from looking up at him.

When the ticket appeared from the slot, she took his money and fed the ticket through the gap in the counter. "Enjoy the film."

"I will," he said, his head bowed as he stepped away from the counter, past all the tempting popcorn and confectionery, and moving towards the theatre.

Following the crowd, he tagged onto the end of the queue and waited. Tapping his foot impatiently, he listened to two women in front of him giggle hysterically about an incident that had occurred at work. *What's the bloody hold-up? Why can't everyone just find a seat and be done with it? Because they want to sit together. Pathetic people, they can't talk to each other during the movie, so why make a fuss about sitting together?*

The usherette also seemed annoyed at the situation. He wanted to tap her on the shoulder and ask which one of the group he should kill next. He was sure by the expression on her face that she would be tempted to go along with his plan.

Eventually, the group was seated. The usherette beckoned him to join her and pointed for him to sit close to the back—he wouldn't be choosing his own seat this time. As more people filled the cinema, his breathing became more erratic. He could sense the opportunity to kill his next victim slipping away.

In the end, he found himself seated between a young couple arguing under their breath on one side, and an old woman constantly dipping her hand in and out of a large crisp packet on the other. The incessant noise was causing his annoyance level to tip dangerously towards choosing her as his next victim.

Once the movie started, she had the decency to stop eating the confounded crisps. That turned out to be the briefest of respites, however, when she tore open a bag of sweets and began either noisily smacking her lips or crunching on the damn things.

His hand slipped into the carrier bag at his feet, and he caressed the length of the blade, tempted to remove the knife from the bag, in spite of the close proximity of the arguing couple, and insert the blade in the woman's side. He imagined twisting it endlessly until she choked on the confectionery that was driving him nuts. However, he thought better of it and counted to fifty to help calm his anger.

Two hours later, the film ended, and the crowd began to disperse. The arguing couple left their seats first, leaving him alone with the old woman. He caressed the blade of the knife again, but he restrained himself. She shifted in her seat, trying to elevate her rotund body. Although killing her would please him, it wouldn't give him the same satisfaction the other murders had. He would need to remain patient, for now. There would be other opportunities in the near future—that much was guaranteed.

He waited until nearly everyone had left, then he exited the building. The rain pelting his face stimulated his desire to punish someone again.

"Any spare money for me to buy a cuppa?" A homeless man begging on the corner opposite caught his attention. "Thanks very much, guvnor, much appreciated."

Several people dropped coins—their hard-earned money—on the soggy coat in front of the man. His heart rate escalated when the man smirked at their gullibility once their backs were turned. At least that's how he read the situation. A eureka moment entered his mind.

Heroic Justice

This man would be his next victim—this con artist *deserved* to be the next one on his list.

After another ten minutes, the area was clear of lingering cinemagoers. Making sure he kept in the shadow of the nearby building, he approached the man. "Hey, would you mind giving me a hand with my car? I could do with a push to get it going. There'll be twenty quid in it for you."

The homeless guy's eyes narrowed, peering through the darkness to see who was talking. He shrugged and got to his feet.

Yes, that's it, come to Daddy.

He turned his back, and the man followed him into the nearby alley.

The man shouted, "Hey, I don't see no car down here. What's your game, buster? I'm out of here."

The voices in his head started bickering, trying to decide what he should do as the man turned on his heel and retreated. His target had only managed to go a few steps before he pounced on him. His knife gripped firmly in his right hand, he drew it across the homeless guy's throat. Within seconds, blood seeped from the gaping wound and mixed with the puddles of rain pooling beneath them, declaring that the man's useless life had ended. Placing the limp body on the ground, he walked away from the scene, stooping to pick up the handful of cash lying on the guy's coat as he passed.

"Every little helps!" he muttered as he strode away from yet another murder. His fourth and counting. He grinned. *I could get used to this.*

CHAPTER TEN

Lorne stretched and picked up her mobile to look at the time. "Damn, Tony, we've overslept. It's almost eight o'clock."

Tony groaned, and she shoved him out of bed. "Get up, you lazy sod. You take longer than I do to get ready. Shoo—get in the shower, quick."

"What a charming good morning that is from a loving wife."

"Sorry, you know how much I love you. You also know how much I detest being late. Now shift."

She watched Tony attach his prosthetic leg and hobble to the bathroom, riddled with guilt that she'd probably hurt him when she'd ejected him from the bed. "Is your leg all right?"

He turned to smile and proceeded to walk properly the rest of the way to the bathroom. "Of course, I love pulling your leg, though. Boom boom!"

"Ha-bloody-ha! I'll get you back for that prank when you least expect it."

"Promises, promises," he shouted above the noise of the shower.

Lorne sifted through the clothes they had discarded and rushed over to the wardrobe to hang up the garments before she selected her navy-blue trouser suit and cream blouse. She draped them on the bed and returned to the wardrobe to find a suitable ensemble for Tony, to save him some time and to make up for kicking him out of the bed.

Tony entered the bedroom, grinning. "Don't you trust me to dress appropriately around your new friends, dear?" He pouted a little then roared at Lorne's mortified expression and her blustering to find the right excuse.

"Umm... it's called being wifely and helping you out."

"Right. You keep telling yourself that, love. I'd call it a guilty conscience myself."

"I don't have time for this. Wear what I put out, or don't, see if I care." She ran into the bathroom, jumped in the shower, did her best to avoid getting her hair wet and was out again within seconds. She brushed her teeth and applied a limited amount of makeup before she returned to the bedroom to find Tony wearing the clothes she had chosen for him. "Glad you saw sense in the end."

"It was either that or put up with evil looks all day."

She scowled at him while putting on her own clothes. "You can be such a liar at times."

He placed a hand on his chest and raised an eyebrow. "*Moi*?"

"Yes, you. Are you ready? We can grab a coffee at the station. Maybe there's a baker's close by where we can pick up a bacon roll or something."

"Did you have to mention a bacon roll? Now I'm salivating."

"Shall we leave the car here and get a taxi to the station?"

"Makes sense to me. We can hitch a ride with Nelson if we need to go anywhere. I'm sure he won't mind."

They left the hotel and flagged down a taxi driving past the front door.

When they arrived at the station, the desk sergeant recognised them, asked them to sign the register then called one of his staff to show Lorne and Tony up to the incident room on the next floor.

Lorne entered the room to find the staff looking quite animated. Hero appeared in the doorway of his office and shouted across the room. "We've got another victim, Inspector. Grab a coffee, and I'll fill you in before we shoot over to the scene."

Tony veered off towards the vending machine while Lorne made a beeline to join DI Nelson. "Same MO?" she asked, entering the room.

He motioned for her to take a seat. Tony entered the room a few seconds later and handed Lorne a coffee, then they both sat forward in their chairs as Nelson filled them in.

"Same cause of death—a knife wound to the throat—however no longer in the cinema, like the others."

Lorne and Tony exchanged puzzled glances. "Where did the attack take place then?" Lorne asked.

"In an alley. Close to a cinema, though," Hero said.

Lorne's eyes narrowed. "Hmm... I wonder what spooked him to change his routine."

"Something did, obviously," Hero replied.

Tony shrugged. "It's hard to get a feel for what happened without viewing the scene. Why don't we ease off with the speculations until we get there?"

Hero nodded. "Agreed. I'm going to ring the pathologist, see if she's still at the scene." He picked up the phone, punched in a number, and put the call on speakerphone. "Susan. Hi, it's DI Nelson. Just wondering if you're still at the location."

"Hi, Hero. Why are you being so formal? Yes, I am. Getting ready to pack up, so you better get your skates on if you want to meet me here."

"Sorry, yes, we'll be right there. I'm bringing a couple of detectives with me. They've come up from the London area, got them on speakerphone now, so no slagging off the southerners, like you usually do." Hero chuckled.

"Ha, as if I would. Nice to know that you have such a high opinion of me. Right, see you soon."

"We're leaving now." Hero hung up.

"She sounds a right scream," Lorne said, amused.

"She is. We get on very well together. Not sure many DIs can say that about the pathologist they work with."

"I have the same rapport with the pathologist in my area. She's become a good friend of mine through the job."

~ ~ ~

Twenty minutes later, they arrived at the cordoned-off crime scene, where Hero introduced Lorne and Tony to Susan Rendell. The woman greeted them with a smile in spite of the intense pressure she was under.

"There was a witness, right?" Hero asked Susan.

"I believe so. Uniform dealt with that side of things, not us. He was long gone by the time my lot arrived."

"We can chase that up," Lorne said, surveying the area high and low.

Hero nodded. "Any ID on the chap?"

"Surprisingly, yes. Even though he was homeless, I found a blood donation card in his pocket."

"Wow, really?" Lorne reached for the evidence bag Susan got out of her case.

"I thought it was incredible, too. Obviously, we don't know this guy's background. Sometimes, especially nowadays, just because someone is living on the streets, it doesn't always follow that it's their fault. Perhaps he just fell on hard times, had his home repossessed or something along those lines."

Hero pointed his finger. "Good point. I'll ring Julie, get her to do a background check on him, see if anything comes up. We'll need to trace his next of kin anyway."

Lorne handed him the man's blood donation card, and he walked a few feet away to place the call.

"You're from the big smoke then? What brings you up here? The case?"

"Yep, we've had two similar crimes on my patch. As soon as I heard about the third victim dying in the same circumstances in Manchester, I rang DI Nelson. I'm not averse to sharing the glory on this case—that is, if we catch the bastard. It's proving difficult with no evidence found on any of the four victims."

"I'm in touch with your pathologist in London. We'll put our heads together, virtually, if we have to. Hopefully something will show up soon enough."

"Fingers crossed. Otherwise, this guy could carry on killing until the world ends."

"Right, my job is finished here. Back to my gaff to perform the PM."

Hero joined the group again. "Julie did a preliminary search for me while I was talking to her. The guy was recently divorced. Looks like his wife has remained at the house with the two kids."

"Damn. We're going to have to let her know what's happened if there are no other next of kin on the radar." Lorne's mouth twisted with uncertainty. "Why don't I see what the cinema manager has to say about things? My take is that he went to the cinema before he killed Jim Hamilton, if only because of the time the incident happened."

"Good idea. I'll go through things with Susan and catch up with you in a few minutes."

Lorne and Tony walked towards the cinema and knocked on the front door.

The young man who had been watching the SOCO crew from his position in the foyer rushed to open the door for them.

Lorne produced her ID. "DI Lorne Warner. Are you the manager?"

"Yes. Come in. What a dreadful incident to happen on our doorstep."

"I agree. Mind if we ask you some questions?"

"Me? About the incident? Not sure I can help you, as it didn't occur on our premises."

"Granted, however, it could have done. The local DI investigating a crime similar to this put out a TV appeal last week. Did you not see it?"

The man's eyes widened, and he shook his head. "No, I didn't. I tend to work very long hours and don't seem to find the time to watch TV. But anything you need, I'll be more than willing to help."

"We appreciate that, Mr...?"

"Tyler. Jake Tyler."

"Can you tell us how busy the cinema was last night?"

"I've just looked at the takings, and we appear to have had a really good night compared to this time last week."

"I don't suppose the staff who were working last night are on duty yet?"

"No, they won't arrive until around elevenish."

"That's a shame. Maybe we can call back later today to interview them. We need to find out if they saw or heard anything out of the ordinary."

"I can ring the supervisor who was on duty after I left at eight, if you like?"

"That would be brilliant, thank you."

Tyler dashed into a room off to the left and returned carrying his mobile phone. He punched in a number. "Hi, Cathy, it's Jake. I have the police with me about an incident that took place across the road from the cinema last night. Do you know anything about it? Hang on, I'll put you on speaker so I don't have to repeat it."

"Hi, Jake. I was locking up with Michael at around eleven thirty last night just as the police arrived. I tried to find out what was going on, but the uniformed officer told me to move on. What happened?"

"Someone was murdered."

The woman gasped. "My God, seriously?"

"Yes. The thing is, the police are here wanting to know how busy we were last night and if anything untoward occurred."

"It was mega busy last night. I had to lock the doors at eight thirty as all the seats were taken."

Lorne digested the information. *The doors were locked at eight thirty, but the crime wasn't committed until around eleven. Or did the killer strike earlier than that? Perhaps the body wasn't discovered for quite some time?* She ran through all the relevant questions that needed answering before they could figure out what the killer's routine was.

"Okay, thanks for that, Cathy. And you can't think of anything strange which happened inside the cinema last night?"

There was a slight pause followed by a long breath. "No, nothing that is coming to mind. I've only just woken up, so my head isn't the best at this time of the morning."

"Not to worry. Thanks for your help. I'll see you later." Tyler hung up and shrugged. "Sorry, from the horse's mouth."

Lorne spotted Hero racing up the steps of the cinema. "Can you open the door for my colleague?"

The manager rushed to the door and turned the key. "Sorry, come in." Then Tyler remained by the door while they discussed the case.

Hero smiled at Lorne and Tony. "Anything that we can use?"

"Apparently the cinema was full to capacity last night, and they closed the doors at eight thirty."

Hero frowned. "The timing is out. The victim wasn't discovered until gone eleven. Unless..."

Lorne tilted her head, intrigued to hear his opinion. "Go on?"

"Unless the murderer got locked inside."

"I was wondering the same thing. The other murders took place when the cinemas were less busy. The attacks were committed from behind the victims. Maybe our killer chose people on their own on purpose. People who sat in isolated seats, away from other customers. It would make sense. Less chance of him being discovered either before he carried out the deed or afterwards. I'm fishing at present, I know."

"It looks like that's all we have to go on for now," Hero agreed. "So the killer got locked in, the opportunity to kill someone didn't present itself inside the cinema, so he took his frustration out on a poor homeless guy opposite after everyone had left the area."

"Looks that way to me. Just like the other victims, this guy was in the wrong place at the wrong time."

"So how do we stop him?" Tony asked, his tone flat.

"By not giving up. We need to keep the pressure up. He's cute. He hides his tracks well. We have no DNA evidence that we can use," Hero stated, sounding equally dejected.

"Hey, guys, that kind of tone isn't going to help us. We need to remain positive. Hero, I think we should hold another press conference, a joint one. Let the bastard know we're onto him and that it doesn't matter if he changes city to carry out his heinous crimes—we won't stop until we've caught him." Lorne punched a fist in the air, to raise their spirits. It also proved that she meant business. "Furthermore, we need to question the witness ASAP, if that's all we've got to go on right now."

Hero nodded then turned to face the manager. "Do you have CCTV cameras facing out onto the street?"

"I do. I can copy the disc for you."

"Brilliant. It might give us a lead at least."

With the disc in hand around ten minutes later, they left the cinema.

Lorne paused at the bottom of the steps. "I just want to walk the scene if that's okay with you, Hero?"

"Of course. SOCO have finished with the alley now."

Lorne entered the alley and placed her thumb and forefinger around her chin. "How did he coerce the victim to follow him into an alley—or did he?"

Tony and Hero looked at her then at the entrance of the alley before their eyes settled on the bloody patch on the ground where the victim was found.

"Haven't got a clue," Hero replied.

"He must have tricked him in some way. I know I wouldn't take off after a stranger if that stranger was leading me into an abyss like this," Tony suggested.

Thumping her thigh, Lorne said, "Yet more questions we don't appear to have the answers to. It's all bloody frustrating, and this guy is sitting back, laughing at us."

"Not for long. Why don't we go and question the witness and then return to the station to conduct the press conference?" Hero said, leading the way out of the alley towards his vehicle.

Tony nudged Lorne in the ribs. "Don't give up, love. Between us, we'll get this bastard."

"I'm not so sure, Tony. In fact, I've never been less confident about anything in my life."

CHAPTER ELEVEN

The witness, Patrick Holden, worked at a factory close to where the incident happened. Because his shift didn't start until midday, he was at home when they arrived. He showed the three of them into the lounge while his wife went through to the kitchen to prepare the coffee.

In the car, they had agreed that Hero should lead the questioning. Once everyone was seated, he began, "Thank you for agreeing to see us, Mr. Holden."

"My pleasure. Please, call me, Pat."

"Okay, Pat. Can you tell us what you saw last night?"

Pat fidgeted in his seat. "To be fair, as I told the officer at the scene, I didn't really see much."

"That's okay. Anything is better than nothing at this stage."

Pat wrung his hands together as his wife walked into the room and distributed the mugs of coffee. "Is it all right if Caroline stays?"

Lorne smiled. "Of course it is."

Caroline sat on the sofa close to her husband and rested a hand on his thigh. "Don't be nervous, love."

Pat smiled weakly at his wife then inhaled a large breath. "Well, I had just finished work and was on my way to the car park to collect my car when this man came out of the alley. I couldn't get out of his way. He came hurtling out of there. I suppose I was in a world of my own. You know how it is—you tend to switch off after a long shift."

"I do." Hero replied. "Did he stop to apologise, or carry on walking?"

"If anything, he upped his speed and soon disappeared out of sight."

"Was he carrying anything?"

Pat took a moment to think back. "Yes, I seem to recall he was holding a carrier bag in his right hand."

"Did you get a close look at the man's face? Could you tell if he was wearing a mask?" Lorne asked.

"No, I couldn't see his face. It was very dark, plus he was wearing a hat. It all happened so quickly. I waited until I could no longer see the guy before I ducked into the alley to see why he was making such a hasty getaway. Crap, kind of wish I hadn't bothered now. Those images will stay with me the rest of my damn life."

Hero nodded. "It's not easy being confronted by a dead body. Sorry you had to experience that. Did you call the police straight away?"

"Yes. I was struggling to breathe properly and desperate to get some fresh air, so I left the alley, got out my phone to ring, and that's when I noticed the car coming around the corner. I don't know why, but instead of seeking help, I sank back into the shadows. Good job I did because I think it was the killer in that car. I swear, my heart was beating so damn fast, I thought I was going to croak there and then."

"What made you think the car belonged to the killer?" Lorne asked.

"It slowed down as it approached the alley. I figured he was checking to see if the victim was dead, like the poor guy is going to live through those ghastly wounds." He shook his head in disgust and reached for his wife's hand, gripping it tightly until his knuckles turned white.

"So, the car slowed down. Did the driver get out of the vehicle?" Hero asked.

"No. He stayed there for a moment or two, although it felt like a couple of hours at the time, then he drove off. I got on the phone to the police then in case he came back. I was tempted to run off without bothering to ring it in, if I'm honest. My conscience refused to allow that to happen, though."

"You did the right thing," Hero said. "Now, can you tell us what type of car it was?"

"I can't be certain about this, but I think it might have been a Ford Granada. It was that kind of shape anyway."

"The colour?"

"Black. Definitely black. Or maybe it was a dark blue. Bugger, I'm doubting myself now... Lord knows what you must think of me. I'm sorry."

Heroic Justice

Hero shook his head. "There's no need to be sorry. It must have been a terrifying experience for you."

"It was. It still is. God, I don't think I'll feel safe again until you catch this person. Oh God, I've just had a thought—what if he comes after me?"

Lorne smiled at the petrified man. "In our experience, just to put your mind at rest, that's highly unlikely."

"Thank God for that. I hardly slept a wink last night."

"I can vouch for that," his wife said, patting the top of her husband's hand.

"Is there anything else you can add?" Hero asked. "Did you get the registration number on the vehicle? Or perhaps you can tell us which direction the car was heading in?"

"Not really. There are a lot of roads leading off Drummond Way. I would hate to mislead your investigation by saying I knew when I haven't got a clue."

"Not to worry. We're going to put out a TV appeal this afternoon."

Pat's eyes almost dropped out of his head.

Hero raised his hand. "No need to panic. We won't be mentioning you. I can promise you that. Only the car's colour and make."

"I understand. Sorry I couldn't be much help."

"Nonsense. Maybe you can give us a brief description of the man, his height, his build perhaps?" Lorne asked, encouraging the man with a smile.

Pat paused as he thought. "My height and build, but that's as much as I can give you on that front, what with it being so dark. Sorry."

"No problem. What about what he was wearing? You mentioned a hat. What type of hat?"

"He wore one of those floppy hats. I think he was also wearing a casual zip-up jacket and jeans."

"Any distinctive smell, like a cologne or personal hygiene issues?"

"No. I'm sorry, I feel so useless."

"There's no need to feel inadequate. Every minute detail helps. You've been brilliant. The main thing is you've identified his vehicle—that's far more than we've uncovered ourselves. Right, we better get back to the station. Thanks again for your assistance, and please, try not to worry about this man seeking you out. We'll ensure a patrol car circulates the area frequently for the next few days."

Pat Holden let out a relieved sigh and rose to his feet to show them out. He shook hands with the three of them as they left. Lorne noticed how sweaty his palm was and held on to his hand a few seconds longer as she assured him, "Please, just go about your normal routine. We'll catch this man soon. I promise."

"I hope so, Inspector. People like that should be locked up and never see daylight again." He closed the door quietly behind them.

"At least we've got the vehicle's make and colour to be going on with and a guesstimate of his shape and build," Tony announced, getting in the rear of Hero's car.

"Yeah, plus we have a rough idea what time the incident occurred... but nothing else at this point," Hero mumbled as he slid behind the steering wheel.

Lorne remained silent on the journey back to the station. She kept going over and over what Holden had told them, frustrated that the man hadn't taken notice of the killer's face when he'd barged into him.

Hero organised his team swiftly when they arrived back at the station. Jason informed him that Julie had gone to visit the victim's ex-wife to inform her of his death as no other relatives could be found through the system.

"Okay, that's good. Right, Jason, CCTV footage of outside the cinema. I want you to trawl through it. I have no idea what angle it features, but our witness says that a black Ford Granada slowed down at the end of the alley. Looks like that's the killer's vehicle. Let me know what you find, Jason; we need a licence number to go on ASAP."

"I'll see what I can do, sir."

Hero returned to where Lorne and Tony were standing. "There's not a lot we can do now until we go before the cameras. Why don't you guys go out and grab some lunch?"

"If it's all the same to you, we'd rather stick around here," Lorne replied hesitantly.

"I've got a compromise for you to consider," Tony piped up. "Why don't Lorne and I go to the nearest baker's and pick up some rolls for the team?"

Hero smiled his appreciation and pulled out his wallet. "Sounds like a plan to me. Here's twenty. That should cover it. I'll be in my office, preparing what I need to say to the public in a few hours."

"We won't be long. I'd like to give you a hand with that, if you're agreeable?" Lorne said.

"Of course. I'll make a start."

After getting the orders, Lorne and Tony left the station and went to the nearest Greggs, returning half an hour later, laden down with rolls and a mixture of yummy doughnuts to satisfy the hard-working team.

Lunch out of the way, Hero invited Lorne to take a look at his notes to see if she wanted to add anything—she didn't. So they made their way downstairs to confront the media gathered in the special conference room. The TV company had booked a slot on ITV to air the appeal live. Journalists from other TV companies and the newspapers were all present, too.

~ ~ ~

The killer was flicking through the portable TV that had been in the house when he'd broken in. The house was rundown and unloved, and it hadn't been lived in for a year or more, judging by the size of the cobwebs in every corner of all the rooms.

A police appeal caught his attention. He listened intently as a male and female inspector addressed the public. *Ah, so they've joined forces, have they? It's going to take two smartarse inspectors to take me down, is it? Well, we'll have to make this a bit more interesting now.*

He approached the mantelpiece and glanced at his reflection in the cracked mirror. Catching sight of himself for the first time in a while made him flinch. Not so long ago, his face had been one of his best features. He'd been almost Hollywood handsome until...

The voices started up in his head, blocking out the sound of the TV. *You're an ugly fuck! They did this to you! You should punish them. Punish them all! They let you down when you needed them the most. It's payback time!*

His eyes narrowed. The voices were right. Only he could alter his future. He had nothing left of his past now, except the scars that did their best to remind him of what he'd put himself through, what they had forced upon him.

Turning away from the mirror, he sat down on the worn-out couch and pulled the tab on a beer. Downing the can in one long gulp, he focused on the two detectives. Their desperation was clear. "They only have my car, no plate number, just the make and model. There must be hundreds of thousands of black Granadas out there. They won't find me. I won't allow it to happen. Not yet. I've been careful so far. Maybe I should start leaving a few clues. They're obviously too dense to solve the crimes and could do with the help. Well, I'm more than willing to oblige on that front. She's a bit of all right, the female detective. Older than I thought at first. Been round the block a few times, would be my guess." He laughed until his sides hurt as the appeal was opened up to questions.

"Why do you think the killer has altered locations?" a male voice asked.

DI Nelson replied, "We have no idea. To be honest, we know very little about the killer. But we're hoping that the public will help us out now that we've identified his car."

"Have you, though? Identified the car? You have the make and model, but you'll need more than that to make an arrest surely, Inspector," the same journalist asked.

"Granted. But it's more than we had yesterday. Just a moment..." The male detective covered the microphone in front of him with one hand and placed the other hand up to cover his mouth as he leaned sideways to talk to the female detective, who nodded. "What we can also tell you is that this man wears a mask to carry out the attacks."

The crowd muttered loudly before a woman journalist asked, "Why are you only just revealing this fact, Inspector?"

"We need to keep something up our sleeve, Milly."

"Very well. What makes you believe he's wearing a mask? Can we ask what type of mask it is?"

"We have CCTV footage of the man wearing what appears to be a latex mask that is pretty lifelike. That's all I can give you at this point. Any other questions?"

The crowd muttered again, but no one raised a hand to be heard.

"Okay, then I'm drawing this meeting to a close. I'd like to thank you all for attending and would just like to say how much we appreciate you covering this case for us in the media."

The appeal ended, and the screen went back to the anchor woman in the studio, who recapped what little evidence the detectives had mentioned.

"They've got nothing. They're utter prats. They have absolutely no chance of catching me as things stand, so it's time to up your game, Robbie boy."

The voices in his mind re-emerged to urge him on. He took out his mobile phone and pulled up Google Maps. It was time to get back on the road again, anything to keep the police on their toes. Time to start changing his MO. He'd been too easy on them, but all that was about to alter.

First, I need a little snooze. I could have a long night ahead of me. He lay down on the couch, a huge grin on his face. Tiredness enveloped him quickly, but the nightmares soon disturbed his sleep, the same as they always did. Huge bangs, men shouting, shots being fired. The noise of battle filled his mind.

The voices coaxed him to go out and kill again. He knew that if he didn't give in to them, they would make him suffer even more. Killing people silenced the voices for a while. He wondered how many he would need to kill for the torment to end. He had no idea, but he had every intention of achieving his aim, no matter how many lives he had to take to do it.

CHAPTER TWELVE

Lorne and Tony gathered along with Hero's team in the incident room to discuss the case as they waited for the calls to flood in from the appeal that had just gone out. The telephone rang a couple of times, but the team could tell right away that they were the usual hoax calls. At six o'clock, Hero dismissed everyone except Jason, who had volunteered to stay behind to answer any calls that came in overnight.

"It's all sorted," Hero announced to Lorne and Tony. "I've rung Fay, and she told me to drag you back home with me for some dinner. How's that?"

"That's really generous of you. Thanks, Hero. We'd love to accept. Is there anything we can bring?"

"Just yourselves. It's only pizza. Hope that's okay?"

"Just the ticket, mate," Tony said. "We appreciate it."

"We'll go in my car. I'll either drop you back to your hotel later or call you a taxi."

The three of them bid farewell to the rest of the team and set off. Lorne felt a little apprehensive in the car about meeting Hero's wife and family. *Would the children even be up when we get there? Of course they will—it's not the dark ages.*

As soon as the front door opened, they were bombarded by excited kids, but Lorne's attention was drawn to Sammy, Hero's adorable Rotti cross. Sammy rubbed himself against her leg, and she scratched his back as he moaned appreciatively.

"He'll be glued to you for the rest of the evening now, Lorne." Hero laughed and picked up his children one by one, kissed them, and spun them around.

"I don't mind. I love dogs. And who is this?" She ruffled Hero's son's hair.

"This is our eldest, Louie. Say hello to our guests, children. Go on, introduce yourselves."

Heroic Justice

"Why don't you conduct the introductions in the living room, where there's more room, love," Fay said, leaning against the doorframe.

Lorne smiled. "Seems like a good idea to me. You must be Fay." She shook the woman's hand. Hero's wife oozed friendliness. "Good to meet the lady behind the great detective at last. Gosh, you do have your hands full here. I only have the one, and she's twenty-two now. I can't believe I said that. Makes me feel so old."

Fay led Lorne into a comfortable lounge. "Excuse the mess, but make yourselves at home. Oh, and, Lorne, you don't look old enough to have a daughter of that age. I hope I look as good as you at your age, although with this mob around me, I can't see that happening."

"It must be hard work. Hero said you work from home, as well. I find that incredible. Well done, you."

"It'll be easier once the twins are at primary school—that'll be in September. They're really good kids, to be fair, compared to some of the monsters I see tearing out of school at the end of the day."

Lorne watched Tony latch on to Louie and Hero. Louie had set up a game on his Xbox and the men were caught up in the world of fantasy within seconds.

"Shall we leave them to it?" Fay sniggered and walked into the kitchen.

Lorne followed her. "What a charming house you have. I love this kitchen. It's much bigger than mine. Have you been here long?"

Fay filled the kettle then rested the small of her back against the worktop and folded her arms. "Around five years. It was in a bit of a state when we moved in. I insisted we should tackle the kitchen first. Not sure men prioritise that enough when they're considering renovating a house."

"That's true. It's the heart of the home and should always be given top priority. I'm with you on that one."

The twins entered the room, their arms laden with toys. "Now play quietly, girls. Don't go pestering our guest."

"We won't, Mummy," Zoe and Zara said in unison.

The kettle began to boil. "What does Tony drink, Lorne? Tea or coffee?"

"We're both coffee nuts, I'm afraid. Can I help at all?"

"Nonsense. Take a seat. Everything is under control. We'll eat in half an hour, if that's all right?"

"Sounds perfect. I hate taking people for granted, so please let me help."

"You can lay the table then. How's that?"

"Great. I'll do that now, and then we can have a natter without the boys being around."

"I'll take the drinks through and be right back." Fay carried two mugs into the lounge just as a large cheer broke out. "For goodness' sake, you frightened the life out of me and were almost wearing your drinks instead of drinking them. Do you have to shout like that?"

"Sorry, love. We'll tone it down a bit," Hero replied, grimacing.

Lorne shook her head. Tony seemed to be so relaxed, and it had been a long time since she'd seen him that way away from home.

Fay walked back into the room, opened the cutlery drawer, and deposited the silverware on the covered table. "That's for later. Now, tell me all about how you met Tony? Hero said it was through the job, which I find fascinating."

Lorne glanced over at the twins playing happily in the corner. "I'll brush over the nasty parts because of tiny ears listening."

Fay laughed. "They'll be too engrossed to hear anything anyway."

"To be honest, when I first met Tony, I didn't really warm to him. He was an arrogant MI6 agent, and I was on the hunt for a notorious killer in London. I'd been trying to track the bas... the vile man down for over eight years. Tony had him on the radar, too. My team and I stepped on his toes in an undercover operation, and I had to suffer his wrath. He summoned me to meet him in a secret rendezvous, all very cloak-and-dagger stuff."

"Oh, how exciting. Is that where love blossomed between you?"

"Hardly, he was quite abrupt, but he discovered that the Unicorn had coerced one of my sergeants into sleeping with him and to acting as his mole. She'd lied to the entire team for months."

Fay's hand covered her mouth, and she shook her head in disgust. "Crikey, that's the pits."

"I know. It really left a bad taste in my mouth. I took pleasure in arresting her, slung her in a cell, but the Unicorn sent his solicitor to the station to give her a capsule of cyanide. When we discovered her body, I didn't know whether to feel anger or pity for the woman. She must have been desperate to have considered suicide." Lorne pointed to her head. "It still affects my decision making today. I know it shouldn't, but it's really hard finding staff you trust. That's why I have such a small team compared to other MITs."

"I think Hero suffers from the same issues. His partner is in line for a promotion. Between you and me, he's never got on that well with her, but he's dreading the day he has to replace her with someone new."

"Better the devil you know, eh? His team seem really good, though. I can't say I've had much to do with Julie since we arrived."

"I just think she's misunderstood most of the time. I've not dealt with her much. I try and tell Hero to not be so hard on her. She had problems caring for her mother, and that also often interfered with the job. Sadly, she passed away a few years ago, and I think Julie is still devastated by that. Hero also detests her on-off boyfriend, as well. Lord knows why."

"Oh dear, sounds like Hero needs to distance himself a little. He appears to be a very caring man. Just seeing how he interacts with his family tells me that much. Not every copper I know goes home after a long stressful day and starts playing with his kids as soon as he walks through the door. He's to be admired."

"He's lovely. Taken a major emotional hit lately after the death of his father... we all have. Even the kids are still getting emotional not having their grandfather around," Fay said, lowering her voice so the twins wouldn't hear.

"I lost my dad four years ago. He was an integral part of our family, too. He lived with us, an ex-copper. This villain I was talking about kidnapped him, doused him in petrol. Tony, my DCI and I managed to rescue him before the Unicorn's goons struck the match. Dad sort of declined after that day. He would never have agreed with that statement, but I could see it in his eyes. Something in him died that day. He helped me set up and run the rescue kennel, but that soon took its toll on him physically. Once Charlie—that's my daughter—was old enough, she begged me to let her take over the everyday running of the rescue centre. She was good at it, too. She's such a brave girl, the bravest young lady I've ever met, considering what the Unicorn put her through."

"Blimey, that criminal must have really had it in for you. Did he go after your daughter, too?"

Lorne nodded as unexpected tears filled her eyes. She whispered, "He raped her and forced her to work in the sex trade along with other young girls, most of them foreign who he'd trafficked into the country."

Fay placed a hand to her cheek. "My God, how dreadful for all of you, especially your daughter. I hope you caught him and made him suffer?"

"I ended up retiring from the force. I told my DCI that the Unicorn was still alive after he believed he'd been killed in an explosion, but my gut instinct said otherwise. It was Tony who proved me right. He convinced me to go to France with him to track the bas... the sadistic swine down."

"You're a braver woman than me, Lorne. Was that the end of it?"

"Yes. The police would never have been able to deal with him. It took three MI6 agents to put an end to him, but even that task put my life in jeopardy. After that, Tony and I became inseparable. You have your Hero, and I have mine. Even the Taliban couldn't destroy what we have."

Fay shook her head and frowned. "Taliban? How were they involved?"

"Tony was on a covert mission in Afghanistan, and the Taliban captured him." Lorne lowered her voice. "The short story is that they chopped one of his legs off."

"Goodness me. Your family have certainly been through a tough time in one way or another over the years, Lorne. I'm so sorry about that."

"It's awful, but we've come through it—that's the main thing. Together, we're stronger because of the trauma that's been flung at us. What I'm trying to say in a roundabout way is that Hero will overcome the death of his father eventually."

"I know he will. He was very close to his dad, though—we all were. He was one of life's charmers. Never fell out with anyone and did all he could to help people out if they were in need."

"It's harder the nicer our parents are."

"I agree. It's a shame you don't live up this way, Lorne. I think we'd all become firm friends."

Lorne smiled. "I think you're right, Fay. Hey, there's nothing to stop that from happening. You and Hero can come and visit us with your tribe one weekend, if you don't mind bunking up together, that is?"

"We'd love that. Let's get dinner out of the way and the kids settled in bed and have a natter afterwards."

"Deal." Lorne laid the table while Fay saw to the meal itself. The aromas filling the kitchen made Lorne's stomach grumble. "It smells delicious."

Heroic Justice

"Do you want the works? Pizza, chips and beans? You're not one of these women on one of those faddy diets, are you?"

"Nope. I eat anything and everything. I suppose the stress of the job helps to burn off the calories if I ever eat too much."

"Good, what about Tony? Shall I give him a large portion like Hero?"

"Go for it. I'm sure he'll eat what's on his plate. He does at home, even when he cooks a meal."

"Wow, how did you manage to train him to do that? I need some tips. Hero is beyond useless in the kitchen."

"Truthfully, Tony used to be. He once cooked spaghetti without using any water in the pan, ruined my copper-bottom pot. He's come a long way since those days. He really is one in a million. He works full time as a PI, too, don't forget."

"Blimey, I definitely need to have a word in someone's ear in that case."

They were both still laughing when Tony, Hero and Louie walked into the room. "Can I smell tonight's culinary delight, darling?"

"I don't know about culinary delight, love. You can smell the pizza, though. Hey, you and I need to have a serious conversation after our guests have gone."

Lorne cringed and winked at Tony's raised eyebrow.

Hero looked perplexed. "We do? May I ask what about?"

Fay smiled at Lorne. "Lorne's just been telling me that Tony cooks most of the meals in their house."

Hero's mouth dropped open and he stared at Lorne. Recovering, he said, "Wow, and there was me thinking we were getting on really well."

Everyone roared with laughter. As Fay and Lorne dished up the meal, Hero said to Tony, "Hey, bro, you've let the side down."

Fay turned around and glared at her husband. "A *very serious* chat!"

Tony punched Hero in the arm. "Sorry, mate."

The food was yummy, and the conversation during the meal was excruciatingly funny at times. Lorne had forgotten what it was like to spend time with young children at mealtimes. Her sister, Jade, had two young sons, but since Lorne's father had died, Jade had become far more distant. Being around this lively, contented family made her realise what she was missing out on. She vowed to ring her sister at the earliest opportunity once they were home, if only for a catch-up.

After dinner, Hero offered to help Fay bathe the kids and put them to bed. Lorne and Tony volunteered to do the washing up and to tidy up the tornado-hit kitchen. Fay tried to object, but Lorne insisted.

Chores completed, the four adults collapsed into the sofas in the lounge with a bottle of wine. They chatted like old friends about everything under the sun until the conversation changed direction and landed on the case that was causing them problems.

"Maybe someone will recognise the car when they watch the appeal," Fay suggested, snuggling into Hero.

"Let's hope so, because after four murders, we really don't have much. I'm beginning to think this guy likes toying with the police. These murders aren't just about ending someone's life. I get the feeling he's getting some kind of kick out of deceiving us. He's revelling in the knowledge that we have no idea who he is or what we can do to try and prevent him from killing more people," Hero said, the cheerfulness disappearing from his voice.

Lorne nodded thoughtfully. "I'm inclined to agree with you. The question is, how the heck do we go about stopping him? Especially now his MO has changed slightly. We also need to figure out why he's chosen London and Manchester to carry out the crimes."

"That's the worrying part—the change in MO. He could go off at a tangent, kill dozens of people, and we might never connect the crimes. At least when he was killing people inside the cinemas, he was consistent."

Tony sighed. "Maybe you should be looking at the mask side of things?"

Lorne glanced at him and smiled. "You're right. At the very least, it might give us a different direction to take in the investigation. Why does he feel the need to wear a mask? Where did he buy it? There might be a paper trail."

Hero yawned. "I apologise. I think the day is catching up on me."

Lorne patted Tony on the thigh. "We should be going now. It's almost ten."

"Sorry, I didn't mean to drive you away."

"You haven't, Patch. It's been a wonderful evening. Thank you both for being so hospitable. Your family is gorgeous, and you should be very proud to have such well-behaved kids."

Fay beamed. "That's lovely to hear, Lorne. Whether it'll always be this easy, well, none of us can see that far ahead. It's good to know we're doing some things right anyway." Fay hugged Lorne and Tony. "It's been a pleasure having you. Hopefully, we'll be able to do it again soon. Good luck with the case." She kissed Tony on the cheek, and Hero walked Lorne and Tony to the front door.

"I'll get my keys." Hero reached in his jacket pocket.

Lorne placed a hand on his arm. "Honestly, we'll walk, at least part of the way. We'll flag a taxi down in the main street."

"If you're sure?"

"We are. A nice romantic stroll will do us good. See you at the station bright and early, and thanks again for a fabulous evening." Lorne leaned forward and kissed Hero on the cheek.

Tony shook Hero's hand. "Cheers, mate. It's been a fun evening. See you tomorrow."

Hero waved them off then closed the door quietly as they left.

"It's not often you can strike up a friendship as quickly as that. They're a lovely couple," Lorne said, hooking her arm through Tony's.

"Come on, you. Let's hope we find a taxi soon. I have no idea what direction we should be going in."

They shared a brief kiss and laughed then headed along Hero's road to the crossroads at the top, where they flagged down a cab.

CHAPTER THIRTEEN

After a restless night's sleep, he decided to get on the road early. Unsure if he would be heading back this way soon, he packed a holdall with all his belongings. He took one last look around the lounge as a chill ran through. It was a typical September morning, and he made a mental note to choose a house that had central heating for his next base. The two-bar electric fire sitting alongside the thirties' fireplace had given up the ghost years ago.

He unzipped his bag again to ensure he had packed his mask. His head was foggy from lack of sleep, and he couldn't recall putting the latex mask in his holdall. It was there, however, staring up at him. With everything packed, he left his secret hideaway through the back door, the same door that had given him access a few days before through a broken pane of glass.

His mind cleared as he jumped in his car and set off towards the M6. Almost immediately, he wished he'd postponed his journey until after the rush hour had passed. He inserted a Black Sabbath CD to help him kill the time as the traffic crawled along, until suddenly, the motorway was clear ahead of him. He could never figure out how that happened. He hadn't travelled far when a spot in the distance drew his attention. He eased off the accelerator as the object grew larger. His heart pounded, and his mouth gaped open as he tried to calm his erratic breathing.

The girl waved frantically and eagerly ran towards the car as he pulled up at the kerb. "Hi, thanks for stopping."

His eyes remained ahead of him, surveying the area. "Where are you going?"

"London, but if you're not going that far, anywhere will do."

"Hop in. I'm going all the way. It'll be good to have some company."

The girl opened the back door, threw her rucksack in, and hopped in the passenger seat beside him.

Heroic Justice

He selected first gear and filtered into the traffic. "You really shouldn't hitchhike. You never know who might pick you up."

"I know. I don't normally, but I need to get home. My mum is ill, and I don't get paid for another week, so I couldn't afford to get a train like I usually do. I'm so grateful to you for stopping. I didn't relish getting a ride with a truck driver."

"You're safe with me. Do you mind Black Sabbath?"

"No, go for it. I haven't heard any of their stuff for a while."

He turned up the stereo, more to drown out any conversation she might have contemplated having. They drove in silence for the next half an hour. He glanced sideways now and again to check out her slim denim-clad legs and tanned slender arms. His groin pulsed, and his erection grew the more he thought about having her legs wrapped around him.

The traffic had thinned out considerably, and up ahead, he saw a wooded area. He pumped the accelerator pedal, making the car kangaroo jump. "Oh no, not again."

He felt the girl look at him. She turned down the music and asked, "Is everything okay?"

"I just had the mechanic look at her for the same problem. I can't believe it's happened again. I need to pull over and take a look. I know what the problem is, but I can't correct it until I've seen what's going on under the bonnet. Sorry about this."

"It's okay. Do what you have to do. I'm in no rush."

He kept pumping the pedal, making the car judder forward now and again, until he pulled into a lay-by. He switched off the engine. His hand left the gear stick and curled into a fist, which then connected with her face. The girl screamed and reached for the door handle. He pressed the button to apply the central locking system. Then he hit her a second time in the face before he turned in his seat to look at her, revealing the horrendous scarring on his right cheek. Terror filled her eyes, making her wince. Anger steered his next movements. His fist pounded and pounded at her nose. Blood gushed from her nostrils, and she passed out when she saw the blood drip onto the back of her hand.

Patiently, he waited for the road to clear. He unfastened her seatbelt, and when the last car had passed, he darted out of the vehicle and hauled the blonde girl into his arms before another car appeared. He ran for cover. Despite her height, she was lighter than he anticipated, making it easier for him to spring for cover.

He tried not to look at the blood streaking her face. Placing her gently on a pile of dry leaves, he glanced down at her body hungrily.

Do it! Go on, you know you want to! She'll want it too, once you've started. It's been a while. You need to get rid of all those pent-up feelings you have. What better way to do that?

He listened to the voices—they sounded convincing. Then, an idea of his own sparked in his brain. A different kind of crime might confuse the coppers even more. He decided to go with the plan and unfastened his belt. He dropped his trousers then partially tore off the unconscious girl's clothes. It wasn't ideal—he would have preferred her to be awake while he dipped his stick, but he realised that he couldn't have everything his own way.

After doing the deed, he returned to the car to fetch the girl's rucksack. He carried it into the woods and dumped the bag at her feet. With one last lustful look at what he'd just sampled for free, he legged it back to the car. Buckling up his seatbelt, he waited until another vehicle had driven past then pulled out behind it. Switching on the CD again, he drummed his fingers to the beat, a satisfied grin pulling his lips apart as he continued on his journey back to London to cause yet more mayhem for the two inspectors investigating his case. His groin pulsed again when the female inspector's image entered his mind. I'd certainly give her a good seeing-to if ever the opportunity arose.

CHAPTER FOURTEEN

Hero greeted Lorne and Tony like old friends when they showed up at the station at a quarter to nine the following morning.

"What's on the agenda this morning?" Lorne asked, walking over to the vending machine to buy the three of them coffee.

"I have the usual crap to deal with first thing. I wondered if you and Tony wouldn't mind sifting through the telephone messages regarding the TV appeal. I'm sure most of it will be tossed in the bin, however we might be able to use snippets of it here and there."

"We can do that. Are you sure we won't be stepping on your team's toes?"

Hero waved his hand in front of him. "Not a chance. These guys are pretty easy-going. I should be with you in an hour, tops." He walked into his office and closed the door.

Lorne surveyed the team. Julie was watching her, warily, as usual. Lorne approached Hero's partner and tentatively said, "DI Nelson wants Tony and me to look through the results of last night's appeal."

"I was just doing that myself."

"Oh right. Maybe all three of us can do it then."

Julie sighed and handed the pile of notes to Lorne. "Nope, it's all yours. If that's how the boss wants to play things, it's fine by me."

Lorne smiled at the woman. "Can we sit anywhere?"

"Yep. Take your pick. Everyone is at the desk they use now anyway."

"Thanks." Lorne grimaced when she returned to Tony. "Let's sit over here out of the way. I think Hero's partner is a bit pissed off with us."

"Tough shit! If that's what Hero wants, then she's got to accept it."

Hero emerged from his office just over an hour later. He headed straight for Lorne and Tony. "Anything?"

Lorne shook her head, disappointed. "It's worse than we thought. Nothing at all so far."

Hero glanced at his watch. "It's coming up to ten. Maybe we'll get some calls this morning. This is just going to add to our exasperation, right?"

"Yeah, it's not good. Maybe we should look at going down the mask route as Tony suggested last night."

"Sounds good to me. I'll get Sally on that now."

It wasn't until midday that something reared its head. Lorne took the call from an old gentleman by the name of McIntyre. "Hello, sir, how can I help you?"

His voice was shaky. "I was hoping I could help you, dear. I watched the news last night, and it gave out this number if the public could be of any help. Well, I think I can... be of help, that is."

"Regarding the murder case of the homeless man?"

"I think so. In the appeal that young male detective—can't remember his name for the life of me—he said you were looking for a black Ford Granada. Well, I didn't think anything of it at the time, but one pulled up outside my house a few days ago."

Lorne clicked her fingers to gain Hero's attention. He flew across the room to stand beside her. "Sir, I'm putting you on speaker so the investigating officer can hear this conversation."

"Whatever. Don't interrupt me when I'm in full flow, or I'm likely to forget where I was. As I was saying, this car appeared a few days ago. I didn't know who it belonged to. Never saw anyone get in or out of it, until this morning. It's gone now. Sorry to tell you that, but I thought you should know about it anyway."

"That's a shame. And you didn't see anyone either get in or out of the vehicle?"

"Not before today. At around nine this morning, I saw a tall man get in it. Only saw the back of him. Anyway, to me, he was acting suspiciously. If I didn't know any better, I would have said he came out of old Frank's place. God rest his soul, he died this time last year."

Lorne reached for a Post-it and a pen. "Can I have the address please, sir?"

"Walnut Grove. I live at twenty-six, and Frank lived at twenty-eight. That's in Sale, Manchester."

"Would it be okay if we sent someone over to take a statement from you, Mr. McIntyre?"

"I suppose so. I don't want any trouble, though."

"No problem. Would you rather I came to see you?"

"That would be nice. Long time since I've had any female company in my house."

"Just a second. How far is it from here?" she asked Hero.

"We could be there in twenty minutes."

"There you go, sir. We'll see you in twenty minutes, if that's okay with you?"

"I've got a doctor's appointment later, so I won't be able to talk to you long, not that I know much anyway."

"We'll be in and out, I promise."

"See you soon. Bye for now."

The old man disconnected the call. "I think we should get SOCO over there ASAP," Lorne said, rising from her chair.

"I agree. Julie, will you organise that for me?" Hero called across the room.

Julie lifted the phone on her desk to place the call. "They're on their way, sir," she confirmed a few seconds later.

"Good. We'll trundle over there to see what we can find. Hold the fort here, Julie."

"Of course," his partner replied, looking disgruntled.

~ ~ ~

Within twenty minutes, they pulled up outside the row of terraced houses. While they waited for the SOCO van to arrive, Lorne knocked on Mr. McIntyre's house and took down his statement.

He asked Lorne to join him at the bay window in his lounge and pointed out the window. "That's where it was parked, out front. You see, I had a limited view of the man from here. He had his back to me, too, which means I wouldn't be able to identify him in one of those line-up things, before you ask."

"Don't worry. We'll do our best to get him. I don't suppose you caught a glimpse of his registration number as he drove away, did you? That really would be the icing on the cake."

The man shook his head. "Sorry, I didn't."

"Not to worry. If he's been living next door, then I'm sure the forensics team will find some DNA that we can work with."

"I hope so. I'm just sorry I can't be of more assistance, dear."

Lorne touched the man's forearm. "Honestly, you calling us, making us aware that this man has been hiding out next door is just the boost we needed, if it turns out to be the right suspect of course."

"I like to do my best for society. I think the older generation is more likely to do that than the youngsters of today. Am I right?"

Lorne smiled. "Sadly, yes you're spot-on. I do think people of your age are far more observant and law-abiding, shall we say?"

Tony appeared in the doorway. "The SOCO team have arrived."

"That's my cue to leave. I have your details, and we'll be in touch if we need to question you further, Mr. McIntyre."

"Okay, dear. I hope what I've told you helps you arrest this vile individual."

"We hope so, too." Lorne followed Tony out of the house, and they both joined Hero at the SOCO van.

"We need you to search everywhere. It's imperative we get the results quickly on this, guys," Hero said to the two Scenes of Crimes Officers who were donning their white paper suits.

"We'll do our best," the older of the two men replied with a firm nod.

Lorne cleared her throat. "Any chance we can take a look inside the house, Hero?"

"Would you object to that, guys?" Hero asked the two forensic experts.

"Don't see why not." He reached into the back of his van and withdrew three additional paper suits. "You'll have to suit up."

"Brilliant." Lorne stepped into her suit quickly, eager to get inside the killer's recent den. "Come on, you two, make it snappy."

The five of them walked down the pedestrian alley at the side of the property to the rear and entered the back garden.

Tony pointed to the broken pane of glass in the door. "His entry point, I take it."

Lorne nodded. The three of them stood aside to allow the SOCO team to enter the property first. The furniture in the house was sparse and very outdated.

"This place smells musty," Lorne said. "According to the neighbour, the chap who owned the property died last year, so I'm not surprised it smells this bad. Looking at the three-foot-tall grass in the front garden, I can see what attracted the killer to take a chance on this place." She flicked the light switch in the kitchen.

Nothing happened. "No electricity, so he's had to use basics I should imagine—cold water and possibly candles—during his stay."

Hero continued past her into an equally sparsely decorated lounge. Apart from a sofa that sank in the middle and an armchair that looked as if it were suffering from mange, there was nothing to say that anyone had been there since its previous owner.

"This is really disappointing. I'll take a look upstairs." Lorne raced up the stairs two at a time, her suit rustling noisily as she ran. She located the bedroom first. "Yes, up here." She pointed to the hairs on the bare pillow as soon as the men walked in the room.

"Good spot." Hero studied the hairs for himself before the forensics team placed the evidence in a pot and sealed it.

"I'm going to check the bathroom." Excited by what they'd discovered, Lorne rushed out of the room and along the narrow corridor to the bathroom at the rear of the property. She couldn't believe her luck when she saw a worn-out toothbrush sitting on the sink. "There's more in here."

Tony joined her. "Looks like we'll get an ID on the bastard soon enough, love."

"Fingers crossed. It's about time we had a break on this one. Of course, this toothbrush might have belonged to the owner of the house. We should get the results back in a few days."

Hero was standing in the doorway. "I'm confident in saying that SOCO will turn up with plenty of evidence here. Why don't we take a quick tour of the remainder of the house, then leave them to it and get back to the station?"

"I agree. I feel more positive about things now that we have some possible DNA evidence to go on."

After they had looked through the other rooms and finding nothing further, they decided to leave SOCO to the task of finding more evidence.

Hero led the way down the stairs. "I don't suppose the neighbour said if he could ID the driver of the car?" he asked Lorne.

"Nope, he only saw the man's back as he got in the vehicle, so I think that's pretty unlikely."

"Not to worry. We'll have the DNA results back in a few days."

Outside the property, they stripped off their suits then jumped in Hero's car.

~ ~ ~

Back at the station, Hero gathered the team to share the news of what they'd discovered at the property. Lorne noticed Julie's narrowed eyes and couldn't help wondering what the woman's problem was. *Is she jealous that Tony and I accompanied Hero to the house instead of her?* After watching Hero's partner for a few moments more, she decided she couldn't stay quiet any longer. "Is there something wrong, Julie?"

All eyes in the room turned to the woman, who fidgeted in her seat and turned crimson. "No, should there be?"

Lorne shrugged. "I feel as though there's something you want to say."

"Is there something you want to share with us, Shaw?" Hero asked, his brow creasing.

"If you must know, there is. You instructed me to visit the fourth victim's wife, and yet, you haven't even asked me how I got on with that task."

Hero tutted. "How very remiss of me. Consider me chastised. Please inform the team what you learned."

It didn't take Lorne to work out that Julie's problem was insecurity.

Julie nodded at her boss and picked up her notebook from the desk behind her. She cleared her throat and began. "Jim Hamilton and his wife were recently divorced. Their marriage was solid until he reached sixty. His firm sacked him the day after his sixtieth birthday. According to his wife, Jim said they were ageist, didn't have any employees on their books over the age of fifty-nine. Anyway, he found it almost impossible to adjust after working a minimum of sixty hours a week for his employers. She said he used to get under her feet a lot, a lost soul without purpose. Then after a few weeks, he started disappearing during the day and not returning until the early hours of the morning. She tried to get out of him what he was up to, but he simply said he was doing as instructed and staying out of her way. It wasn't until the end of the month, when the credit card bills started landing on the doormat, that she realised what he'd been up to."

"Which was, Julie?" Hero asked, his impatience clearly visible.

"He was gambling. I'm not talking a few hundred pounds a week—he spent thousands. So much so that the house was due to be repossessed. That's when his wife demanded a divorce. At present, the house is for sale, and the building society have given Mrs. Hamilton six months to sell the property before they snatch it back from her."

"Crap. I suppose most building societies would have forced her out by now," Lorne said, shaking her head in disgust.

Julie nodded. "When I told Mrs. Hamilton that her husband had been sleeping rough, she was mortified, broke down in tears. Jim had assured her that he was staying at a nearby bed-and-breakfast so he was still close enough to see the children. It was terrible leaving her in such a state, riddled with guilt about splitting up with him. She believes if she hadn't kicked him out, he wouldn't have been murdered. I have to agree with her there, boss."

"We're not in the blame game here, and what's done is done. Is the wife going to come in and identify her husband?"

"Yes, I've arranged to meet her at the mortuary this afternoon."

"Did you ask if Jim had any enemies?"

"I did, sir, but she's clearly out of touch with her husband's personal life on many levels. What little she could offer, she was obviously grasping at straws." Julie replaced her pad on the desk and looked directly at Lorne.

Lorne held her gaze. Even if Julie had a problem with her, Lorne wasn't about to change the way she did things. They were in the middle of an intense investigation, not on the playground at school. She shook her head and looked away.

"Okay, team. I'm optimistic that SOCO will turn up DNA for us, and then we'll have more to work on, so if you have any outstanding paperwork to do with any recent cases, I suggest you deal with that now, while we're waiting on SOCO's report."

The team returned to their computers, and Hero approached Tony and Lorne. "How are you getting on with the calls from the appeal?"

Lorne gestured to a stack of notes. "McIntyre was the only real lead."

"I have a shitload of paperwork I'd like to contend with while—"

Julie spun around in her chair. "Sir, I've had a call from the control room—there's a report involving a black Ford Granada. A rape victim, Kelly Fallon, is in the Manchester Royal Infirmary.

She was hitchhiking and got picked up by a man driving a black Ford Granada on the M6 this morning. The driver assaulted her and left her in the woods at a lay-by."

Lorne turned to Hero. "We should go to the hospital to interview the girl, quickly."

"Sod the paperwork—that can wait. Let's go."

Lorne, Tony and Hero rushed out of the station and jumped in Hero's car once more. Within minutes, they pulled up outside the hospital and raced inside.

Hero and Lorne produced their warrant cards for the receptionist and asked to be directed to where the victim, Kelly Fallon, was being cared for.

"She's in a private room on the women's ward. End of the corridor, take the lift up to the second floor, and it's the first ward on your right."

"Thanks," Lorne said, rushing ahead of Hero and Tony to get in the lift. A silence accompanied them up to the second floor. After exiting the lift, they applied the antibacterial gel then stepped onto the ward. Lorne flashed her warrant card at the nurse on duty, who showed them into Kelly's room. When she heard the door open, the girl's eyes shot open, and she gathered the sheet in front of her.

Before either of the men could enter, Lorne placed a hand on Hero's arm and looked at Tony. "I'll go in alone if that's okay? The poor girl is likely terrified of men right now."

Hero tutted. "I agree. I'll trust you to deal with this, Lorne."

"Great. I'll try not to be too long, but I also don't want it to seem as if I'm rushing her. She needs to take her time. Why don't you guys go grab a drink?"

She watched Hero and Tony walk away, inhaled a large breath, then pushed open the door.

When Lorne entered, the teenager's terrified gaze drifted to the nurse, and her hand tightened on the sheet.

"It's okay, Kelly. She's with the police," the nurse said gently. "Would you like me to stay?"

Kelly nodded, and the nurse smiled. "I'll be right over here," she said, picking up the clipboard from Kelly's bed. She moved to the corner and occupied herself with filling in the chart, in an effort to give Lorne some privacy.

Heroic Justice

Lorne approached the bed and smiled down at the bruised young woman. "Hello, Kelly, my name is Lorne Warner, and I'm a detective. I'm here because I've been working on a case involving a man who drives a black Granada like the one you reported. Are you up to telling me what happened to you?"

The young girl released the grip on the sheet and nodded.

Lorne withdrew her notebook and pulled a chair closer to the bed. "In your own time, can you tell me how you were picked up today?"

Kelly's shaking hand swept over her face a few times as she tried to grasp the words. "I know I was stupid. I was forced into it, really."

"He forced you into the car?"

"No. Sorry, it's my mum. She's sick. I couldn't afford the train."

"So, you hitched a lift?"

"Yes. I feel so stupid. I admit it was a reckless thing for me to do. If I wasn't so desperate, I wouldn't have done it. I never dreamed..." Tears swam in her eyes and toppled past her eyelids.

Lorne smiled encouragingly. "There's no rush. In your own time. I appreciate how difficult this must be for you."

Kelly turned to face her. "Do you? Have you ever been raped?"

Lorne sighed. "My daughter was. I understand the anger and the humiliation it entails. I also know what a great healer time is."

"Your daughter got over it?"

"Yes. I'm not saying it was easy, but she managed to block out the bad things that happened to her and get on with her life."

"And what about boys? Did she learn to... trust again?"

"In time. She has a wonderful, caring boyfriend now."

Kelly let out a shuddering breath. "I'm not sure I'll ever be able to trust another man again. Why? Why do they do this?"

"Each case is different, love. Majority of the time it's about domination. Usually, they feel the need to take their frustrations or their inadequacies out on a woman, and any woman will do. I'm truly sorry you've been through this ordeal. This is not your fault, so don't blame yourself. With your help, we can put this man away. That is, if you're up to talking."

"I... I close my eyes, and all I can see is his face... and the scars."

Lorne sat forward in the chair. "Scars? On his face?"

"Yes, I didn't notice it when he pulled over. He opened the window, but didn't turn all the way to look at me when he spoke. I didn't think anything of it at the time."

"Does that mean the scarring was on the right side of his face?"

"Yes. All the right side was disfigured by this huge scar. Apart from that, he seemed okay, not that he spoke much before he pulled over."

"What kind of scar was it? Was it similar to a burn scar or a deep cut?"

"A deep cut, maybe as if someone had run a knife down his face."

A monitor beeped urgently elsewhere on the ward, and the nurse quietly excused herself.

Lorne nodded her thanks then asked Kelly, "Did he mention where he was going perhaps?"

"Yes, he said he was going all the way to London. I told him that Mum was in hospital and that I didn't make a habit of hitchhiking. He seemed genuinely sorry about my mum. Even said that it wasn't safe to hitchhike. Which confused me when he did what he did."

"I'm not surprised. Sometimes people give you a false impression so that you trust them."

"I fell for his trick. I keep trying to wrack my brain to think if I triggered anything by saying something stupid, but we didn't really speak at all. He was playing music really loudly."

"There's no point blaming yourself. It'll make you crazy in the end." Lorne jotted information down in her notebook, then asked, "What made him stop the car? Did he offer an excuse or just pull over without warning?"

She shook her head gently. "The car started playing up. He said he needed to fix it, that it had been in the garage a few days before but looked like the same problem had struck again."

"Could you tell there was something wrong with the car? Was there a strange noise perhaps?"

"The car started to lurch forward and then appeared to lose speed. Thinking about it now, I bet he did it on purpose, placed his foot on the accelerator and removed it again. Kangaroo petrol, I think my dad used to call it when I was growing up."

"I'm with you. What happened next?"

"He pulled over to the side, in a lay-by close to the wooded area, and hit me in the face. That's the last thing I remember—he hit me over and over. The bastard broke my nose."

Lorne surveyed the purple bruising to both her eyes and the split halfway up her nose. "I'm so sorry, love. Have the doctors told you that it will heal okay?"

"Yes, they said it was a minor break. I never knew there was such a thing."

"Neither did I. I'm glad there won't be too much damage externally for you to deal with. I take it you don't remember anything else about the attack?"

"No. I woke up in the woods after he…" Fresh tears escaped her eyes, and she looked down at her hands as they twisted the sheet beside her. "I'm not sure how long I was out, but when I woke up, my trousers and underwear were down by my ankles, and he'd ripped my shirt open. My bra was up around my neck. I felt dirty and violated. He'd had the decency to leave my rucksack beside me. I knew I had to change my clothes before I searched for help. I'd left home in such a rush that I forgot to charge my phone, so the battery was dead. That only left me with one other option—to flag down another car. Do you realise how traumatic it was for me to do that?"

Lorne nodded, imagining the fear the young woman must have been dealing with at the time. "You were brave beyond words. I'm not sure I could have done the same if I were in your shoes."

"I kept picturing my mum's face. I needed to get to her. I was determined to get back to London, but I've failed."

A thought struck Lorne, and without checking out the details first, she announced, "I can see if we can get you transferred if you like?"

"I'm not sure how long they expect me to stay here. If they release me, I'll be in the same situation. I can't afford the fare to London and would be forced to hitchhike again."

"No, you won't, love. I can organise either a transfer for you or get one of our guys to take you down to London if you'd prefer?"

"You'd do that for me?" Kelly asked, shocked.

"Of course. Our role as police officers is to protect the public, and that duty comes in many guises."

"I need to get to my mum. She needs me."

Lorne nodded. "Your first priority should be to yourself, to let your wounds heal before travelling anywhere."

"I know, but she doesn't have long left. She has lung cancer, you see."

"I'm sorry to hear that. Please don't worry. I'll get something organised for you soon. Did the man mention what part of London he was going to, by any chance?"

"No, he didn't tell me. Do you think he's attacked other women... you know, the way he attacked me?"

"Not that we know of. We're investigating him for entirely different crimes. We only discovered recently what car he was driving, and we were following up on the car's description rather than the crime. Still, the more you can tell us about this man, the more likely it is that we will apprehend him—and keep him from committing further crimes of any nature."

"He's a monster... all I keep thinking is that he's going to come after me, to finish me off. Is that normal in instances like this?"

"I doubt that will happen. If it'll help we can offer you some form of protection until the criminal is caught."

"You're allowed to do that? I thought that kind of thing only went on in bad American films I've seen."

Lorne smiled. "I've seen a few of those myself. I assure you, we have the resources to do that over here, too. What about looking through some mugshots? Do you think you'd be up to doing that, Kelly?"

"I think so. I want to help all I can. I think it'll help me in the healing process, too."

"I'm sure you're right. If you can give me a brief description for now, we can start circulating it and gather up the relevant mugshots. And I don't suppose you managed to get a look at his number plate?"

"No, I'm sorry. I'm sure I did, but I didn't commit it to memory, and my mind is too fuzzy to recall it. The man's description is different, though—every time I close my eyes, it's all I can see. He's there in front of me, as if he's taunting me somehow."

"Okay, in your own time." Lorne poised her pen over a blank sheet in her notebook and waited patiently for Kelly to begin.

She closed her eyes, and fresh tears dripped onto her cheek as she forced herself to recall the man's image. "He had quite a long, thin face, like he hadn't eaten properly in months. His eyes are a vivid blue, his nose is a little misshapen, broken perhaps—I know that feeling now, thanks to that cu... pig."

Lorne smiled as she watched the girl's expression run the gamut of emotions. "You're doing so well, love, please go on. What about his mouth or lips? Thick or thin?"

"Thin, like the rest of him. His chin was rounded, not pointed. That's all I can remember about his facial features. His hair was a light brown, lighter than mine. It was short, as though he prefers to shave it rather than have scissors shape it—am I making sense?"

"Perfect sense to me. Go on, you're doing really well."

"From what I could tell, he was quite tall. Obviously, he was sitting down in the car, so I can't give you his exact height. I'm five ten, and I suppose he was a few inches taller than me, if that helps."

"It does. You're brilliant at this. Most people wouldn't be able to recall half of this information, Kelly."

She opened her eyes and smiled briefly at Lorne. "That's it. Will it be enough to catch him?"

"I'm sure it will. You're an absolute star. One last thing... did you pick up any kind of accent?"

"I don't think so. I'm not really good on accents unless they're really broad, like a Brummie. My best friend is from Birmingham, and I sometimes find it difficult to understand what she's saying."

"Again, you've told us something we didn't know already, which is all I can ask."

"I'm glad. I'm very tired now." Her eyelids began to droop.

"I can understand that, love. I'm going to see what I can do for you about a transfer to get you closer to your mum, and I'll have one of the local officers come round with photographs for you to look at. Of course, the transfer will be dependent on what your doctor says."

"Thank you. I really do appreciate all your help. I was at a loss what to do about getting to London. I'm sure the stress would have hindered my recovery, but knowing that you're willing to help me has alleviated that stress. I can't thank you enough."

"It's my pleasure. I'll be in touch soon. Try and rest now."

Kelly smiled and waved as Lorne left the room before the girl's head hit the pillow.

Hero and Tony rushed to hear what Lorne had to say. "Well?" Tony urged.

"Right, here's the deal. Hero, we need to do what we can to help this young lady. She's given me a great description of her assailant and is willing to look through mugshots if you'll arrange that."

"That's fantastic. We can get onto that ASAP."

"Okay, I also think we should offer the girl some form of transport. She was forced to hitchhike through lack of funds. Her mother has lung cancer, and she was desperate to visit her in hospital in London."

"What a shame. Again, we can sort something out for her as soon as the doctor gives us the all-clear. How was she? After relaying what had happened to her?"

"She'll be fine. She's a strong character. If she'd been timid, I doubt she would have been able to come up with the fantastic information she has given me." She showed him her notes and looked at her watch. "We should get back to the station now."

"My thoughts exactly." Hero strode off towards the lift.

"Are you all right, love? I know questioning the girl must have stirred up memories you'd rather have kept suppressed."

"You're spot-on, as usual, Tony. I'm fine, though. I told her about what Charlie had been through, and it seemed to break the ice, made her open up quicker than I expected her to. Look, I think we need to head home soon. The girl said the man was on his way to London."

"Shit! What are we waiting for? We should go now."

They reached the lift just as the door opened. "Everything all right, guys?" Hero asked as they all got into the lift. "Why the serious looks?"

"We need to return to London, Hero. Kelly said the man was heading that way."

"Damn, he's on the move. After what he's done to this girl, who knows what he's going to do next. He's becoming unpredictable, and I don't like that."

Lorne nodded. "I despise it, too."

"Can you ring Katy? You should make her aware of his movements," Tony chimed in.

"I'll do it in the car. Damn, I should have checked in with her before this."

As soon as the lift doors opened, they rushed out to the car, which Hero had parked on a grass verge.

Once settled on the backseat, Lorne fished out her mobile and dialled Katy's number. "Hi, hon. It's me."

"Bloody hell, there was me thinking you'd forgotten all about me after dropping me in the shit."

Lorne cringed. Her partner's jovial manner was missing from her tone. "Sorry, it's been hectic up here."

"Ditto. Thanks to you leaving me with a mountain of paperwork to sift through. I have a constant headache that is impossible to shift, while you've been up there gallivanting."

"Whoa, do you want to take a breath there, partner, and calm down a little? We've been doing nothing of the sort. Actually, I was ringing up to inform you that we're on our way back."

"Good. Because I've had it with this shit, Lorne. There's a reason I asked for demotion, and that crappy paperwork is the prime contender."

"Katy, please, can we leave this until I return? I need to tell you something important, and we're wasting time."

Katy huffed. "Go on, surprise me."

"We believe the killer is on his way back to London. I need you to put out an alert for the patrol vehicles to be on the lookout for a black Ford Granada. I have a rough description for you, too. We think the man is around six feet tall. Light brown hair, closely cut as if shaven, blue eyes, and a gaunt face as if he hasn't eaten in days. He also has a huge scar on the right side of his face, which could be why he's worn a mask to carry out the other crimes."

"You *believe* the killer is on his way back? Do you know who this guy is?"

"We're hoping to have that information in a few days. I'll tell you the ins and outs when we return, love. Just go with the description of him and the vehicle he's driving for now, all right?"

"Okay, I'll action it as soon as I get off the phone. Anything else I should know about?"

"His latest victim is in hospital. He raped her in a lay-by after picking her up hitchhiking and left her in a wooded area."

"The bastard! But these girls ask for trouble when they hitch a sodding ride."

"She was in a desperate situation—I'll fill you in on her details later—we're lucky she could give us such a great description of her attacker. Tony and I will be back in a couple of hours."

"See you then. And, Lorne?"

"Yes, Katy?"

"Sorry for flying off the handle. I've been up half the night with Georgina."

"There's no need to apologise. See you soon."

CHAPTER FIFTEEN

His thirst for action got the better of him. He parked in the multi-storey car park in town and made his way to the cinema he used to frequent as a child. He smiled at the memories. He'd been happy then. Every Saturday morning, he and his older brother, Malcolm, had come to the cinema with a group of their friends. They used to have a whale of a time, although as they got older and rowdier, the manager threatened to ban them all if they didn't tone down their behaviour. They had all thought he was joking, but when one of them brought a bottle of vodka with them one morning, and they started singing loudly along with the adverts they'd seen thousands of times before, the manager took pleasure in frogmarching them off his premises.

 He chuckled as he slid the mask over his face. After waiting on the street corner for a group of people to arrive, he made his way across the street and up the steps to the cinema. He kept his head bowed the whole time he was in the queue. However, he felt someone watching him. He glanced sideways and saw a young blonde girl in staff uniform eyeing him suspiciously. After retrieving his ticket, he slipped his hand into the bag as he walked past the girl. Her eyes never left him, making him feel self-conscious.

 He raced into the theatre and presented his ticket to the usherette, his hand covering his cheek, obscuring her view of the mask. He found his seat quickly and waited until the lights dimmed before he began his search for the next victim. On his left, three rows ahead, a man was sitting alone. He picked up his bag, ducked down, and moved swiftly to the seat behind the man. He barely moved for the next half an hour or so. Once the main film began and the actress's screams surrounded him, he made his move. He reached into the carrier bag and stroked the handle of the knife. That's when the voices started up. *Go on, do it. He deserves it. This is payback, remember?*

Heroic Justice

His heart thundered against his ribs, beating rhythmically like a bass drum. The vibration rattled his body and jangled his nerves. He needed a release, and he knew only one way to obtain that. Despite his urgent desires, he waited for the right opportunity to present itself. Blanking out everything else, he withdrew the knife and watched it glint in his lap, reflecting the images on the screen.

He hadn't made the mistake of going to a new movie this time. He chose one he'd seen at least ten times already, one he knew by heart. It was just coming up to the really loud part, the part he knew would help disguise his actions. Sweat dripped from his palms and ran down his wrist as he raised the blade. The music was building to its crescendo. One glance either side of him told him that all the other cinemagoers were either engrossed in the film or hiding behind their splayed fingers. With one swift movement, the deed was done. He wiped the blade across the man's jacket and watched his head tilt to one side.

Go on! Don't stop there! The voices started goading him. *Coward, you could raise the body count at the mortuary within seconds if you had the guts. Go on! Take the plunge. There! To the right. Move across the row and get behind her. She's ripe for the slaughter! Slit her throat, deep and hard. Make it count. If you do it hard enough, her head will drop off. We'd love to see it roll down the aisle.*

He placed his hands against his temples, trying to squeeze the voices out of his head. He couldn't stand it much longer. Why weren't they satisfied with the carnage he'd already caused? When would they be satisfied? They had driven him to distraction on the battlefield, as well. In truth, that was when they had begun. He'd given them what they had yearned for and killed several enemy soldiers just to shut the voices up. Then his commanding officer had reprimanded him.

Payback. Go on... your whole life has been a waste. You need to pay back all those who have spoken out against you. Prevented you from doing what you wanted to do. Go on! You can get away with doing another one. Do it. No one is watching. It'll make you feel better. Call it therapy! You love a piece of therapy to make amends, don't you? This is it—your therapy!

He shuffled along the row to the seat behind the young woman then waited patiently for his next opportunity to present itself.

He retrieved the knife and slid it onto his lap. Streaks of the man's blood muted the gleam on the blade, but he didn't care. It would be good to have two kills in one afternoon under his belt. The police would be going bonkers soon, desperate to trace him. He wondered if maybe he should ditch the Granada. *Shut up! Concentrate on the task at hand. Do it! Give it to her... hard this time. Rip her head off.*

He grabbed the handle and turned the knife so it was flat. When he was just about to reach around the girl's throat, a man entered the row and locked eyes on him.

"Behind you! Watch out!"

He took off before anyone could chase him, but his leg hampered his running. He bolted up the aisle and through the door, knocking over the girl who had noticed him before he'd gone in to see the movie.

"Stop him!" she called out to her colleagues.

Several of the men tried to grab his arm, but he flashed the blade in their faces.

"Make my day, sonny!"

Every one of the would-be heroes hesitated just long enough for him to pass. Then he heard the screams coming from inside the theatre, telling him they'd already discovered the body.

Laughing, he ran down the steps and crossed the busy road, darting between the traffic, until he made it back to the safety of his car.

CHAPTER SIXTEEN

The second Lorne laid eyes on Katy, it was obvious how much strain her good friend and partner had been under. Tony accompanied Lorne to the station, and he caught up with the rest of the team while Lorne took Katy into her office for a chat. The instant Lorne closed the door behind them, Katy broke down in tears.

"Oh, babe, what's all this?" she asked, gathering Katy in her arms.

"It's so bloody dumb of me. I'm sorry, Lorne. I've felt so out of my depth since you've been away. I can't tell you how relieved I am that you're back at the helm where you belong."

Lorne gently pushed Katy away from her and sat down on the edge of her desk as Katy dropped into the chair. "You should have rung me. I would have come back sooner."

"And what would you have thought of me then? God, what the fuck is wrong with me?"

"Look, stop that! You're being too hard on yourself. You've only been back at work a few weeks. Balancing motherhood with a taxing job is no walk in the park, sweetie. Don't think that you've let me down. I shouldn't have rushed off like that."

Katy shook her head. "Don't think that. Your hands were tied. You were—and still are—trying to track down a serial killer."

"Okay, I'll make a pact with you: if you stop beating yourself up, then I'll push my guilt for dropping you in it to one side, for now." She held out her hand for Katy to shake.

Katy inserted her hand into Lorne's and smiled. "Deal."

Lorne pulled a tissue from the box on her desk and handed it to Katy. "Dry your eyes. Look, I was going to fill you in on what went on up in Manchester, but you look done in. Let's catch-up tomorrow and call it a day now, agreed?"

"Would you mind?"

"Not at all. Come here, give me another hug. I've missed you, Katy, and I'm not only talking about the past few days. I mean since you've been on maternity leave."

Katy walked into her arms and squeezed her tightly. "I've missed you, too. I thought I'd missed being in the thick of things until you forced me into taking up the reins."

"Now don't you go thinking that you can walk away from the job, because I'll track you down and drag you back here screaming if I have to. Promise me that you'll talk to me when you find things getting on top of you."

"I promise. I'm just feeling super fragile at the moment, probably down to the lack of sleep. AJ's brilliant with Georgina during the day, but he's so exhausted at night that he sleeps through her crying, so muggins has to get up and see to her."

"That's so unfair. Parenthood is so overrated in my book. People neglect to see the bigger picture when they have children. Hey, look on the bright side, only another five years, and she'll be going to primary school."

Katy laughed.

"Come on, let's call it a day."

"It's good to have you back. Tony's looking good. I hope you two had time for a bit of romance while you were away?"

"Not really. Hectic time with the case, then Hero Nelson, the DI in charge up there, invited us over for dinner at his place last night. He's got a lovely family, three very well-behaved kids, so there's hope for you yet."

"Don't wish that upon me. I'm having trouble coping with one child for now, let alone bloody three of them. What's the DI like?"

"Much like you and me, if I'm honest. Very capable at his job, unlike other men I've worked with that high up. But don't tell him that if you ever get to speak to him. I wouldn't want his ego to balloon."

They left the office arm in arm, laughing.

"Okay, team, I have lots to inform you about regarding the case, but Katy has circulated the man's vehicle and description to the patrol teams, and that's as much as we can do right now. So let's call it a day for now and go over things methodically in the morning. It's good to be back, guys."

After the team had switched off their computers and left for the night, Lorne turned off the lights and walked out to the car park with

Katy and Tony. She hugged her partner goodbye and waved her off. Exhausted, she willingly let Tony drive home so she could take a snooze.

Carol was crossing the courtyard when they arrived. She greeted them with a broad smile and plenty of hugs. "You've been missed. How was the trip?"

"Not as successful as we'd hoped. How have things been around here in our absence?"

"Tickety-boo, as always." Carol's expression suddenly turned serious. "Any chance I can have a word with you before I shoot off?"

Lorne grimaced. "Sounds ominous. You're not throwing in the towel on us, are you, Carol?"

"Nothing of the sort. I'll pop the kettle on, make us all a much-deserved drink."

"Sounds good to me."

"You two go ahead, and I'll grab the bags," Tony called out.

Lorne followed Carol into the house. "Come on, spill?"

"Sit down, love," Carol said, filling the kettle, then flicked the switch.

Lorne dropped heavily into the chair. "Now you're worrying me. Is it Ted? Is there something wrong with him? Or you? You're not ill?"

"No. Will you hush up for a minute? The spirits have been prodding me, Lorne, urging me to speak to you. I didn't want to do that until they gave me something worth talking to you about."

"Just tell me."

"This killer you're chasing, you need to be extra careful with this one. The spirits are restless. I've never seen them so anxious, if I'm honest. I'm concerned for your safety. Promise me that you'll keep Tony close to you at all times."

Lorne's mouth dried up, and she shrugged. "I'll try, but I can't promise."

Tony entered the kitchen, and Carol and Lorne both turned to look at him.

He frowned, his gaze drifting from Lorne to Carol. "Something wrong? More to the point, have I done something wrong?"

"No. Leave the bags there. Come and sit down," Lorne said to him.

Tony pulled out the chair next to Lorne and sat down. "What's up?"

"Carol has just warned me to be careful and that I need to keep you close at all times."

"Can you give us more than that, Carol? I can't go to work with Lorne every day. I have my own business to run, remember? Anyway, DCI Roberts would come down on us like a ton of bricks if he caught me hanging around Lorne too much at work."

"I know. I'm simply passing on what the spirits are telling me, Tony. They're giving me the sign for danger. This killer I'm sensing is unstable."

"Aren't they all," Tony interjected.

"Yes, of course, but this one is different," Carol said.

"Are you picking up anything specific about the killer, Carol?" Lorne asked, wondering if Carol would tell her about the scarring to the killer's face.

"Nothing really, except he's dangerous. His back is turned at present. I have no idea why. The thing is, I'm not picking up just one murderer."

Tony and Lorne exchanged worried glances. "He has an accomplice?"

Carol raised her hands in front of her. "I don't know. It's all very confused right now. No doubt things will become clearer the deeper you get into the investigation. You know how these things work, love."

"I know, Carol. I'll make sure I'm never alone. Would that put your mind at ease?"

"Yes. I wish I could tell you more. You know how much it frustrates me when I can't give you more than a snippet. I'll try my best to tap into the spirits tonight, although, I'm feeling a little tired this evening. So don't bank on me getting anything out of them."

"You take it easy. There's no rush. Thank you for covering today."

Carol rose from her seat. "It's always a pleasure looking after the little darlings, you know that. Any news on finding a replacement for Charlie yet?"

Lorne chewed her bottom lip before she replied. "No, to be honest with you, I haven't even looked into that side of things. I must sort that out soon. I'll chase up Charlie in the next few days. She was going to spread the word down at the agility club."

"I'm sure someone suitable will come your way soon, love. I'll ring you tomorrow, see how you're getting on. Be careful out there."

"I will. Thanks again, Carol."

Heroic Justice

Lorne and Tony waved Carol off and went back inside. "Hmm... do you think there's anything in what she said about the killer?"

"Do I think he's going to endanger my life somehow—is that what you're asking me, love?"

"In a nutshell, yes."

"I have no idea. You know I always trust what Carol and her spirits have to say. Try not to worry too much, though. Don't forget I have a pretty special spirit guide of my own watching over me." Lorne smiled and kissed him gently on the lips.

"I know. She still scares the crap out of me sometimes. It's the unknown I hate dealing with."

"Right. That's why it's best to take what she says at this early stage with a pinch of salt. She'll let us know when danger is imminent, that's the time we should start to worry. Right, I'm starving. What do you want to eat?"

"Do we have anything in? Want me to nip out for a takeaway?"

"No, I'll rustle something up. I'm too hungry to wait for a takeaway. Trust me, you'll enjoy what I come up with."

His eyes narrowed, but he picked up the bags and left the room without saying a word.

~ ~ ~

Fifteen minutes later, Lorne summoned him to the kitchen. "Enjoy."

He sat down and focused on the plateful of food in front of him. "What have I done to deserve this?" he asked, sarcasm dripping from every word.

"Cheeky sod. Don't judge it until you've tasted it." Lorne watched him take the first mouthful.

He moaned his satisfaction as the pasta slid down his throat. "Wow, this is fantastic."

She smiled and tucked into her own food. The dish—pasta, baked beans and a sprinkling of cheese—had been one of Charlie's favourites when she was growing up.

They were halfway through the meal when her mobile rang. "Hello, DI Warner."

"Ma'am, it's the control centre. We've had a report of an incident at a cinema, and I thought you should know right away."

Lorne's heart sank. She pushed her plate away and rolled her eyes at Tony when he raised an enquiring eyebrow at her. "Okay, you've got my attention. What are we looking at?"

"Thanks, ma'am. One murder and one attempted murder at the cinema in Henley-upon-Thames."

"I'll shoot over there now. Thanks for the call." She hung up and pushed her chair away from the table. "I have to go."

Tony bolted down the last few strands of pasta on his plate and stood up, too. "You're not going anywhere without me, especially at night."

"You don't have to come, love. I'm sure the killer is long gone by now anyway."

"It ain't gonna happen, Lorne. Come on, we're wasting time. I'll ring Charlie, ask her to come back to look after this place."

"But she's out with Brandon, enjoying herself."

"Tough, she won't mind. This is an emergency."

"I'll just grab my handbag, and you can call her from the car."

~ ~ ~

Thirty minutes later, they pulled up outside the cordoned-off cinema. Lorne flashed her warrant card, and she and Tony ducked under the crime scene tape and entered the building. To the right of the entrance was a group of people in uniform.

Lorne walked towards the traumatised staff members. "Is the manager around?"

A young woman wiped her eyes with a tissue and pointed at the door leading into Screen One. "In there... that's where it happened."

"Thanks. We'll be back to speak to you soon."

Tony rushed to keep up with Lorne.

They found a well-dressed young man at the back of the theatre, his arms folded. With one hand covering his mouth, he watched the SOCO team deal with the body. Lorne tapped him on the shoulder, and he yelled.

"I'm sorry," she said. "I didn't mean to scare you."

"Crap! I'm so jumpy after witnessing this. Are you the one who is going to be leading this case?"

"Yes, and you are?"

"Phil Mountfield. I'm the manager here. Have been for the past three years, and I've never had to deal with anything this gruesome."

"Is there somewhere we can talk privately, Mr. Mountfield?" Lorne was desperate to get the man away from the scene so that SOCO could get on with their work uninterrupted.

"It's Phil, please. Yes, we can talk in my office. It's a bit of a tip, so you'll have to excuse the mess. I've just taken delivery of promotional merchandise for the new films coming out next month."

"No need to apologise. We're not here to give you a score on your housekeeping abilities," Lorne replied, trying to lighten the mood.

The man didn't react. He just showed them through to the office that was, as he had already intimated, bulging at the seams with boxes. "Take a seat, if you can find one."

Phil sat behind his desk and opened a bottle of water. He downed half the contents and replaced the top. "I'm not sure what I can tell you, Inspector."

"We'll need to question the staff while we're here. Has anyone mentioned if they saw anything out of the ordinary earlier in the day?"

"Yes, Gemma. She had her suspicions about a man when he paid and walked into Screen One. After the lights went on, that same man barged past her and knocked her over. She's inconsolable because she thinks if she'd spoken out, she could have prevented that man being... killed."

"Is Gemma still on the premises?"

"She is. Do you want to speak to her?"

"Yes. I don't suppose there's a staffroom we can use?"

"There is, but it's in a worse state than this. I could get some of the lads to move some of the boxes to give you more room if you like."

"No, in that case, this is fine."

Phil left the room. Lorne heard him call the girl's name, then he returned seconds later with the blonde girl who'd spoken to Lorne in the foyer.

"Hello, Gemma. I'm DI Lorne Warner, and this is my partner." She thumbed in Tony's direction, but didn't introduce him.

"Hello." The young girl wiped her eyes and swept her fringe back from her face.

"Take a seat. Can you tell us what you saw?"

Gemma glanced up at Phil, who was standing alongside her, and he nodded for her to continue. "A man came in and was acting strangely. I tried to get a good look at him, but he kept his head down."

"Acting strangely how?" Lorne asked.

"Refusing to make eye contact and rushing through the foyer. Most people aren't usually in much of a rush to get to their seats, and they tend to linger to buy confectionery or a drink. It just struck me as odd."

"May I ask why you didn't report this to your manager at the time?"

"Mr. Mountfield was in a meeting, and I didn't want to disturb him. I thought I would tell him once he was free, but then I got caught up in a task my supervisor gave me, and it slipped my mind. I'm so sorry. I feel so responsible." Gemma broke down and sobbed.

Phil rubbed her back.

Lorne felt sorry for the poor girl and appreciated the way her manager was trying to comfort her, bearing no grudge. "Please don't feel guilty. You're not the only person he's slipped past."

"If only I had reported it instead of letting it slip my mind, we might have stopped him for today at least. The man steamrollered me when he left Screen One."

"Were you hurt?"

"Only my pride. He rushed out of here and would have given an Olympian sprinter a run for his money."

"Would you be able to identify this man?"

"I got a closer look the second time, and he was definitely wearing a mask. I did notice he had something wrong with his leg, too."

"He was limping?"

"Sort of, but I was on the floor, so noticed his legs when he was running. As his trousers lifted I could see a piece of metal. At least, I thought it was. Is that possible?"

"Maybe a tag? Would you know what a tag we use to track criminals even looks like?"

"Yes, my friend's boyfriend has one, and it didn't look like that."

The next thing Lorne knew, Tony had his foot on the desk.

He pulled up his trouser leg. "What about this? Did it look like this?"

Heroic Justice

The girl's eyes almost popped out of her head. She gasped then nodded furiously. "Yes, that's it. He had an artificial leg. Oh my God, how do you cope with that? Being a policeman, I mean."

Tony placed his foot on the ground again and chuckled. "You don't notice it after a while."

Lorne smiled at her husband and patted him on the knee, then she turned her attention back to Gemma. "That's definitely what you saw? No fleshy ankle, just the metal of the artificial limb, and you said he ran with a limp?"

"I wouldn't say a 'limp' exactly, just awkwardly. But yes, I think he definitely has an artificial leg."

"Just the one? Or didn't you get the chance to look at the other leg?"

"I think it was just the one. Can't say I noticed the other leg. Does that help?"

"Massively. Is there anything else you can think of?" Lorne smiled at the girl, who closed her eyes with relief after feeling she had let them down. "What about his height? Build? His facial features?"

"Well, he was wearing a mask, at least that's what it looked like to me, or he could have quite wrinkled skin... gosh, I really don't know now. I didn't notice when he entered, but when he pushed me out of the way, that's when I spotted it, but only briefly. I suppose he was about six footish, slim build. I'd say he was pretty strong. He must have been to knock me over like that. I didn't notice his hair as he had a hat on. He wasn't wearing that when he came in, though. Does that help?"

"It does, thank you."

"I hope you capture this person soon. To think he could've killed two people here today, it's just terrible."

"Yes, I know. We need to speak to the person he almost attacked, too. Is that person around?" Lorne asked the manager.

"No, her boyfriend came to collect her before the first uniformed officers arrived. I did manage to convince her to give me her address before she went, though. I thought you guys might want to speak with her." He searched on his desk for his notebook, tore out a sheet of paper, and handed it to Lorne. "I think the other witness did speak to the uniformed officers, but I also made a note of his details. If it wasn't for him shouting out, the girl would have been a goner, for sure."

"Thanks, I'll get in touch with both of them after I leave here. Do I need to see any of your other employees, Mr. Mountfield? Obviously, we'll need everyone to make a statement over the next few days, but did anyone else see anything that might prove important in our investigation?"

"I don't think so. Has anyone mentioned anything to you, Gemma?"

"No, nothing."

"I would like to have uniformed officers speak to all of the staff as soon as possible, if that's acceptable to you? They can return tomorrow to follow up with anyone who managed to slip out before we arrived."

"That's fine. When will the forensics team be finished?"

"They should be done in a few hours, and then you'll be free to clean up the area."

"I'll ring head office, see how they want to go about cleaning up. There was a lot of blood on the nearby seats from what I could tell."

Lorne and Tony stood up and squeezed past the boxes towards the door. Lorne shook hands with Gemma and the manager. "Thank you both for all your help. I'm sure it'll make a difference to our enquiry. If any of your staff who were on duty have already gone home, please let them know they'll be required to give a statement tomorrow."

"I'll tell them. Hope you find the culprit soon, Inspector."

"So do I," Lorne mumbled under her breath. She and Tony walked through the foyer under the gaze of the staff and out of the building.

"Do you want to chase up the witness and the girl tonight?" Tony asked, jumping behind the wheel.

Lorne looked at the clock on the dashboard. It was almost nine o'clock. "No, it's too late now. I'll ring them and ask if they can come into the station in the morning. If not, Katy and I can visit them. Let's get home. It's been a long day and I need my comfy bed."

"At least you have some new evidence you can look into tomorrow."

"Yeah, but I would prefer to have the DNA evidence report back with a bloody name for this little shit."

CHAPTER SEVENTEEN

Despite feeling dog-tired when she flopped into bed, Lorne had a turbulent and fitful night's sleep. Every time she closed her eyes, she imagined the killer's masked face taunting her. *If only Carol could have given me something definite to go on...*

In the morning, Tony crept up behind her in the kitchen and wrapped his arms around her waist. "Morning, beautiful. I see you were awake half the night."

She twisted in his arms to face him. "Sorry, love, did I disturb you?"

"It doesn't matter. Don't let this guy get to you, Lorne. You're better than that. You'll catch him."

She sighed heavily. "I have no doubts about that, but how many more lives are going to be lost before we bust this guy?"

"Not many, I hope. I need to get off soon, see how Joseph has been coping without me." He kissed her lips firmly. "Don't be too hard on yourself, love. You're doing your best given the clues and evidence you have."

"I know. I need to shoot off now, too. I'll just have a quick chat with Charlie before I go. See you later. I'll be expecting a cordon bleu meal tonight." She laughed when his face dropped.

"I better grab a takeaway in that case." He rushed out the back door before she could throw something at him.

She made a fuss of Sheba, waited for Tony's car to leave the drive, then let her loyal companion out. "Come on, girl, let's find Charlie."

As Lorne walked into the kennel block, the resident dogs charged to the front of their cages to greet her. Charlie was at the end of the run, lugging a heavy sack of food from cage to cage, placing a scoopful in each dish for the dogs.

"Hi, love, I just wanted to drop by and say goodbye."

Charlie tilted her head and eyed her suspiciously. "You did? Any special reason?"

"No, none at all," she lied. Carol's warning was still twirling in her head. She knew she was being overprotective of Charlie, but if something else ever happened to her daughter because of her job, Lorne would never forgive herself. "I'm going now. Take care. Ring me if you need to, okay?"

"Ah, I get it. There's another madman loose in the area, and you automatically think he's going to go out of his way to track me down, just like... before."

"There are no flies on you, is there? I just want you to be more vigilant than you usually are. Humour me, please?"

"All right. If it'll put your mind at rest, Mum. Now, go, or you'll be late."

Lorne smiled, blew her daughter a kiss, and turned to walk out.

"Oh, Mum," Charlie called after her. "I love you."

Lorne carried on walking, too choked to respond as tears swam in her eyes. She told Sheba to stay with Charlie and closed the door to the kennel before she jumped behind the steering wheel of her car.

Katy was at her desk when Lorne arrived at the station. Her makeup hadn't managed to conceal the dark circles under her eyes.

Lorne bent down and hugged her. "No offence, but you look rough, love."

"Thanks. Lack of sleep again. Third night in a row I haven't had a full eight hours. AJ and I are at a loss what to do next with her."

"Have you rung the clinic for advice?"

"Every day. They told us to take her temperature and to monitor the situation."

"Does she have a high temp?" Lorne asked, stepping back to perch on the desk behind her.

"No. Nothing of the sort. She sleeps well for the first few hours, but when midnight strikes, she's wide awake and remains that way until at least five. Then it's near impossible for me to get back to sleep. In case you haven't realised, I'm getting all my excuses out of the way now before I screw up during the day."

"You won't. You're too much of a professional to do that. I really don't have a clue what to suggest if the clinic can't advise you. Why don't you call the NHS helpline next time, see if they can help?"

"Crikey, I'd feel as guilty as sin if I did that. They have enough to deal with as it is without guiding me through trying to get the little tyke back to sleep."

"What about trying to keep her awake longer?"

"Delay her bedtime? Hmm... I never thought of that. I was beginning to wonder if she's a devil child, you know, what with waking up at the witching hour on the dot every night."

Lorne laughed at the seriousness on her partner's face. "Tell me you're joking?"

Katy's mouth turned down at the sides and she shrugged. "Nope, I'm deadly serious."

"If that's the case, then maybe you need the services of a vicar rather than a nurse or doctor."

Katy's brow furrowed.

"To perform an exorcism," Lorne explained.

"Blimey, do you think so?"

"No, Katy, I was pulling your leg. I'm sure, given time, little Georgina will settle down and let you return to your normal sleep pattern."

"In other words, I need to stop whining about it, and let it take its natural course."

"I didn't say that, but you know I'm always available for a chat. And try not to get worked up about it too much. The more you react, the more she's likely to play you up. At least, that's how I think it works. It has been too long since I had to deal with shit like this. You have my sympathies though, remember that."

"Thanks. What's on the agenda for today?"

Lorne could tell Katy was as keen to change the subject. "Well, you're aware that another murder was committed yesterday. The killer almost murdered a second victim while he was there, too. We need to speak to the witness who prevented the attack and to the lady who escaped the attempt on her life. I want to hold a meeting first thing with the team, and we'll dish out chores then. Alas, I need to check out any paperwork vying for my attention before then. Let me know when the team arrive."

"Okay, I think you'll find the paperwork pretty much up to date, except for what's landed on your desk today."

"You're a treasure. Want a coffee?"

Katy stood up. "I'll get them."

Lorne walked into her office and started tearing open the wad of brown envelopes on her desk. Katy deposited her cup of coffee, smiled, and closed the door behind her when she retreated from the room.

Ten minutes later, Katy poked her head around the door. "Everyone is accounted for. Ready when you are."

"I'm coming now." Lorne gathered the notes she'd jotted down at home in preparation for the meeting and left the office. The team were gathered around in a small half-circle. Lorne stood alongside the whiteboard and began, "By now, you're all aware that the killer claimed yet another victim last night in Henley, almost two, in fact. I'm still awaiting the ID on the victim from the pathologist, but I'll be chasing that up first thing. However, we need to speak to the woman who was almost his second victim and the witness who prevented the attack. Any volunteers for that job?" Lorne asked, her gaze homing in on Graham.

"Okay, I'll raise my hand, boss," Graham replied with a smile.

"Good, because, Karen, I need you to do some important detective work for me on that wonderful computer of yours."

"What's that, boss?"

"When Tony and I questioned the staff at the cinema last night, one of the usherettes said she was pushed over as the killer escaped and got a good look at his legs. She thinks he has an artificial leg."

"An artificial leg?" Katy asked, her voice rising a couple of octaves.

"Yep, and, Karen, I know it's a long shot, but is there any way we can find out if there's a register for people with artificial limbs in the London area?"

"I'm sure there must be somewhere. I'll do my best to locate it, boss."

"Right now, our description of the killer is that he's rather average, except for the scars on the right side of his face and the artificial leg. DI Nelson in Manchester did contact me to inform us that the witness there didn't see a match among the mugshots she was shown. So, until the DNA results from the house in Manchester come back, all we have on our killer are the scars, the artificial leg and the black Granada, but no licence number. It's not much to go on, but it's more than we had a few days ago. Right, let's get cracking, peeps."

Heroic Justice

Katy followed Lorne into the office. "Anything specific you want me to do?"

"Wait a sec, I need to ring Patti to see if we have an ID on the latest victim yet." She picked up the phone and dialled the pathology lab's number. As soon as Patti answered, Lorne said, "Are you free to talk? It's Lorne."

"Of course. Sorry I missed you at the scene last night. I got held up on another job. A pile-up on the other side of town. I didn't get to the scene until gone ten."

"No problem. Have you got an ID on the chap yet?"

"Yes, Brian Carlyle. He's thirty-two. I have an address for you taken from his driving licence. Hopefully, it's up to date. Sixty-eight, Fordyce Road, Henley-on-Thames."

"That's brilliant, thanks, Patti. Have you heard from anyone in Manchester? Any DNA or forensics evidence from them?"

"No, it's all gone quiet. Do you need me to poke them up the arse for you?"

Lorne chuckled. "Would you? We're awaiting the DNA results from a house we suspect the killer treated as his base up there. We also have DNA recovered from a rape victim, and we're hoping it's a match to our killer. At least we think it's the same offender because he had the same type of car and a similar build. By the way, we've found out last night that he has an artificial leg."

"Okay, not sure what you expect me to say about the leg. No jokes coming to mind at this end. I'll do my best to urge them to get a wriggle on the results. Speak soon, gotta fly."

Lorne was left staring at the phone in her hand. "Well, that was short and sweet," Lorne said to Katy. "She's gonna kick the Manchester pathologist up the arse. We should venture out to see if the victim has any family at the address."

"I'll get my jacket."

Thirty minutes later, after tackling a snarl-up on one of the busiest roads in the area, Lorne drew her car to a halt outside a smartly presented, newly-built terraced house. Her knock on the front door remained unanswered.

"Maybe he lived alone. Or his wife is already at work."

"I made a quick call before we left to Missing Persons, and they hadn't received a call last night. Not that it necessarily means anything. The wife might be away visiting relatives or on business.

Who knows? I'm inclined to think he's single, though. Let's see what the neighbours can tell us."

Lorne pointed for Katy to try the house on the left while she knocked on the front door of the other house. A young blonde woman balancing a toddler on her hip answered the door.

"Hi, sorry to trouble you. I'm DI Lorne Warner of the Met Police, and I wondered if you could give me some information about your neighbour." Lorne thumbed next door, indicating which neighbour she was enquiring about.

"Oh right, Brian. Is he in some kind of trouble?"

"No. Is he married or living with a partner?"

"No, he's single. Only lived here six months. What's going on?"

Lorne sighed. "He was murdered last night. I'm trying to locate his next of kin. Did he have any that you know of?"

The woman bit down hard on her lip and rested her head on her daughter's. "Oh my. How terrible. I really can't help you. We haven't said anything more to each other than a brief hello now and again."

"Any idea where he worked?"

"At a bookie's on the high street. That much, I do know. Maybe they can help you."

"Any idea of the name? I should imagine there are quite a few down there."

"Try Ladbrokes. I can't be definite, though. Sorry."

"No problem. Thank you for your help."

Katy joined her but looked equally disappointed. "Anything?"

"No. That's the trouble with these new estates—no sense of community spirit."

Lorne and Katy jumped back in the car and drove down the high street. After parking on double yellow lines outside the shop, Lorne left Katy in the car and went inside. Despite the time—only nine thirty in the morning—the place was heaving with punters watching some kind of foreign horse racing. She walked through the crowd of men to get to the counter, where she flashed her warrant card at the young man with the pockmarked face. "DI Lorne Warner, are you the manager?"

"No. I can get him for you."

"Yes, do that. Thanks."

The young man rushed the length of the counter and returned a few moments later with a rotund man in his late forties.

"I'm the manager, Max Thomas," he said, sliding his spectacles onto the top of his balding head. "How can I help?"

Lorne glanced over her shoulders at the attention she was attracting. "Any chance I can speak with you privately, Mr. Thomas, away from flapping ears and prying eyes?"

"Of course. Come to the end. I'll open the door for you."

The man led her into his office. "I'm here to ask if you have a member of staff called Brian Carlyle."

"I do. He's usually reliable, but I can't seem to get hold of him today. We're super busy, as you can see, and could do with all my staff here to deal with the customers."

"I have some bad news for you. Brian was killed last night."

The man staggered back against his desk as if she'd physically struck him. "Jesus, you're serious, aren't you?"

"Very serious. I need to get in touch with his next of kin. Can you help me out with that?"

The man sighed heavily and walked over to the filing cabinet behind his desk. "Let's see what we can find for you. His mother lives in Liverpool, his father died a few years back. He was close to his mum, visited her regularly. She's going to be gutted about this," he said as he shuffled through the files in the cabinet. "Ah, here it is." He pulled out a file and laid it on his desk. "Poor Brian... was it intentional? Did it happen at a nightclub or something?"

"No, it was during the matinee at the local cinema. He was in the wrong place at the wrong time."

Mr. Thomas shook his head. "What gives people the right to go around robbing nice folk of their lives? It's appalling. I hope you've caught the maniac?"

"Sadly not. Although we're getting closer to finding him by the day."

"Are you saying this idiot has killed before?"

"Yes, we put out an appeal last week regarding two similar incidents in the area, telling people to be vigilant."

"How can people be bloody vigilant? Who knows what type of shits walk amongst us nowadays? Brian was a good man, kept out of trouble, helpful to the punters. Bloody hell, I can't believe he's gone." The man ran his hand over his head and knocked his glasses on the floor.

Lorne picked them up for him. "I'm sorry it's come as such a shock. Can I jot his mother's address down?"

"Of course. I'm not thinking straight, sorry." He handed Lorne the personnel file.

She scanned the page inside, looking for a woman's name. When she found it, she took note of the address and handed the file back to the manager. "I better go now. Thanks for your help."

The manager saw Lorne to the front door and shook her hand. He held on to it for a few seconds and said, "Get the bastard who did this, Inspector."

"I plan on doing just that. Thanks for your help."

Lorne left the shop and jumped back in her vehicle. She placed her pad in Katy's lap. "Do me a favour—ring Merseyside Police and ask them to send someone round there to inform Brian's mother. Request a female officer to do it—you know how insensitive male officers can be at times like this."

Katy nodded and placed the call. Lorne drove back to the station and spent the rest of the day chasing the team for any fresh clues, but there were none.

Just before they clocked off at six o'clock, the phone in Lorne's office rang. "Oops, nearly made it out the door." Lorne turned to the expectant team members lingering near the doorway. "You lot go on. I'll handle it."

All but Katy waved goodnight and left. Katy followed Lorne into her office.

"DI Warner. How can I help?" she answered wearily.

"Lorne, you sound as tired as I feel. Maybe this snippet of news will perk you up."

"Is that you, Hero?"

"Yes. The DNA analysis is back, and SOCO turned up fingerprints at the scene, which finally gave us a name to work with. Thought you'd want to know right away."

"That's brilliant news! Shit, I've just dismissed my team."

"I'll get them," Katy shouted, rushing out of the office.

Lorne's heart fluttered against her ribs. "I've got pen and paper to hand. Shoot me with the details, Patch."

"Robert Lawton."

"And, don't tell me you haven't run a background check on him—I know you better than that."

Hero laughed. "Very good, Lorne. His fingerprints matched his army record. He served in Afghanistan before he received a medical discharge after losing a leg, the damaging facial scars and suffering from PTSD. He's been through hell and back, Lorne."

The word *Afghanistan* sent a shudder shooting up Lorne's spine. Tony had lost his leg in Afghanistan, and every time she heard the country mentioned, she felt bilious. She swallowed down the acid burning her throat. "Okay, that still doesn't excuse his actions, though, Hero."

"Oh, I know. Believe me, I wasn't trying to make excuses for him."

"Sorry, I didn't mean to snap. Crikey, we're getting close now. Have you got an address for him?"

"Yes, he's married, with two kids—a girl and boy, five and seven."

"This doesn't make sense. What the bloody hell would send a family man off the rails like this? His injuries?"

"Maybe. Look, I didn't mention this when you and Tony were up here, but I used to be in the Territorial Army until recently. Retired a few months back. I know it's not the same as serving in the real army, but we still encounter some major atrocities. It's hard dealing with blood and gore—you know that. Crime scenes are one thing, but being in the thick of the action is even more jarring. Maybe it sent him over the edge."

"I suppose you have a valid point. But if blood and gore affected me, the last thing I would do is go on a killing spree."

"You're right. Jesus, I'm at a loss then. How do you want to play this now, Lorne?"

"If you give me his address, I'll go round there. I won't go alone. I'll take an Armed Response Team with me, and that'll take time to organise. Tomorrow might be the soonest I could arrange that."

Hero reeled off the address, and Lorne jotted it down. "Do you want me to travel down there?"

"No, you have enough to do. I can handle it. I'll let you know how we get on. Thanks for the info, Patch."

"You're welcome. Lorne, take care—I'd hate to lose a good friend."

Lorne smiled. "I'm not going anywhere. The Unicorn couldn't bring me down, so there's no chance Robert Lawton will, either."

She hung up and rushed into the outer office. Her team had returned and were looking anxiously at her. She filled them in then rang the ART department. She covered the phone to inform the team,

"They've got a team ready to go. We're going to do this tonight, guys. Are you with me?" Everyone either eagerly nodded or gave her the thumbs-up. She carried on making the arrangements and watched as the rest of her team got on the phone to their loved ones, informing them that they wouldn't be home anytime soon.

With everything organised to hit Lawton's address at seven, Lorne rang home. "Hi, Tony. I'm going to be late. Something has come up that I need to attend to."

"To do with the killer? What?"

"Hero has just rung, and he's identified the killer. An ART is going to meet me at the man's home address at seven. I have no idea how long we're going to be, love."

"Give me the address. I want to be there."

Lorne hesitated briefly before telling him the address. "Let the ART do their job, Tony. Promise me you won't interfere."

"Oh ye of little faith. Of course I won't interfere. I'll see you there."

Lorne hung up. Her intestines had already tied themselves into a jittery restricting knot. "Are we all set, guys? Katy, was AJ okay about you attending the scene?"

"He's fine. Passed on his best wishes to everyone and told us all to be careful. Like we're going to be anything but careful," she said, rolling her eyes.

Lorne laughed. "Okay, we need to organise a plan of what to do when we get there. Karen and Graham, if you go in one car, Katy and I will go in another. I suppose we'll have to wait and see how the commanding officer wants to play it at the scene. Let's hope they don't have to storm the place. I think a reviving cup of coffee is called for before we set off, guys."

CHAPTER EIGHTEEN

The response team had assembled at the end of the suspect's road, and the commanding officer was busy organising his ART experts when Lorne and her team pulled up. Moments later, Tony drew up alongside Lorne's car. She was both relieved and anxious to see him.

Lorne approached the commanding officer. "Hi, I'm DI Lorne Warner, the SIO who rang you."

The broad-chested, five-foot-ten man nodded curtly. "Inspector Dan Styles. I need you and your entourage to stay well back, Inspector. You called us in for a reason. Am I right in thinking that you don't know if the suspect is in the house or not?"

"The minute I found out his address, I rang you. He's killed five people already, so I wasn't about to approach his home without proper support, Inspector."

"We're about ready to go. I need you to stand well back."

"What about the neighbours?" Katy asked. "Shouldn't we ensure their safety before you take action?"

"Let's see where we stand first. There's no point causing havoc if the suspect isn't there. Leave this to us, miss."

Katy shrugged and stepped back to join the rest of the team.

"He's right, Katy," Tony mumbled.

"I know. Wish I'd kept my mouth shut now."

Lorne reached for her partner's hand and squeezed it in her own. "You did the right thing."

The inspector confirmed the address with Lorne before his team swooped into action. Two armed officers snuck up to the house. One disappeared down the side alley that led to the back garden while the other hid by the front door, using the side wall of the house as shelter.

The inspector's voice boomed from the megaphone. "Robert Lawton, we know you're in there. Give yourself up now. We have the house surrounded, and you cannot escape."

Seconds later, Lorne saw a downstairs curtain twitch. "Did you see that?"

"Well, someone is inside, but who?" Tony whispered.

Within moments, the front door eased open. The inspector spoke into his radio.

"Get on the ground, now!" shouted the officer positioned by the front door.

The door opened all the way, and a woman dropped onto the floor. "I'm alone, apart from my children. Please, I haven't done anything wrong. What's this all about?"

The inspector instructed his team to enter the property, then Lorne heard a lot of shouting inside and the sound of children crying.

"Shit, they're terrifying the kids. I don't think he's here. They would have discovered him by now," Lorne exclaimed anxiously.

Tony squeezed her shoulder. "Give them time to search the place thoroughly. It's not uncommon for shits like Lawton to have created a safe place to hide within the property, just in case anything like this drops on them."

The inspector walked towards them as his team emerged from the property. Two officers were holding two young children in their arms. The officer who'd been pointing the gun at Mrs. Lawton helped her to her feet so that she could be reunited with her kids.

"Can I get in there now?" Lorne asked the inspector.

"Yes, my guys have given the all-clear. Looks like a waste of time."

"Sorry, I had no way of knowing if the suspect was at home or not."

He nodded. "Better to err on the side of caution. We'll be getting off then. No doubt you'll be in touch if you need our assistance in the foreseeable future, Inspector."

Lorne shook his hand and turned to the team. "Look, it seems daft all of us being here. Why don't you guys go home? Tony and I can handle this."

"Are you sure?" Katy asked.

"I'm sure. I'll question the wife and see you all in the morning."

Katy hugged her then hitched a ride back to the station with Graham and Karen.

"Are you ready for this?" Lorne asked Tony as they walked towards the house.

"It'll be interesting to see what she has to say for herself."

Heroic Justice

Lorne smiled at the ART officers close to the house. They nodded their acknowledgement before heading back to their vehicle.

She produced her warrant card and showed it to the woman. "Mrs. Lawton, I apologise for the rude interruption to your evening. I'm DI Lorne Warner, and I'd like a word with you, inside if I may?"

"What? Now that you've scared me witless and embarrassed me in front of my neighbours? Yes, come in, let me make you a cuppa and offer you a slice of cake while I down a couple of Valium to calm my nerves." She gathered her children to her again. "Sandy, Carl, let's go inside."

Lorne thought the woman was within her rights to be angry with them.

The children's eyes widened, their glances swiftly moving between their mother and Lorne.

"Please, I can't apologise enough for what just happened, but I'll explain everything once we're inside. I promise."

Reluctantly, Mrs. Lawton guided them inside the house.

Lorne smiled at the woman when they reached the living room. "I really think we should do this without your children present, Mrs. Lawton."

"Well, I don't. They're petrified. If you think I'm going to let them out of my sight, think again. I demand to know why you are looking for my husband."

"If that's what you'd prefer. Personally, I don't think what I have to say should be heard by your children. Maybe they can play in an adjoining room with my partner?"

Tony smiled awkwardly and held his hands palm side up. "They'll be in safe hands. I promise."

"Oh, very well. Kids, can you go into the next room with this man? I'll be as quick as I can. I promise."

"Can we have some ice cream, Mum?" the little girl asked, her mouth twitching into a hopeful grin. Her adorable ponytails and freckles sealed the deal.

"Just one scoop," she said to the girl, then asked Tony, "Maybe you can help her?"

"Of course. Come on, kids, let's go raid the freezer."

The children followed Tony easily from the room, the prospect of ice cream proving to be too much of a temptation in the end.

"Can I sit down?" Lorne asked.

"Yes. Get to the point, Inspector. I want you out of here as quickly as possible."

They sat in the chairs opposite each other in the large, immaculately presented living room that showed no sign of having two young children in residence. "When was the last time you saw your husband?"

"About a month ago. Why?"

Lorne was surprised by the declaration. "A month? May I ask why you haven't seen him for so long?"

Mrs. Lawton sighed heavily. "Because we're separated. Is that against the law, Inspector?"

"No. Can I ask what the reason is behind your separation?"

"Unreasonable behaviour on my husband's part."

"Was he abusive towards you?"

"No, I kicked him out before things got that bad, before he had the chance to lay a hand on me or the children. Although he did threaten me more than once."

"I see. Your husband was discharged by the army, wasn't he? Can I ask for what reason?"

"PTSD. Post-traumatic stress disorder."

The penny dropped. "Did he receive his injuries whilst serving in the army?"

"Yes, in Afghanistan. His regiment was attacked while on manoeuvres. Rob was one of three men injured. A rescue attempt took longer than anticipated. It was touch and go whether he would make it, and they couldn't save his leg. The scarring to his face was what sent him over the edge. Every time he looks at his reflection in a mirror, it's a constant reminder of what he and his army pals went through."

"I see."

"Don't look at me like that, Inspector. I did my best to try and help him, but he's too messed up. He hears voices. They guide his every waking moment, at least that's how it felt sometimes. I could no longer put my kids through that hell. Have you ever dealt with anyone suffering from PTSD? It's no picnic, I assure you."

"I'm sorry if it came across as if I was judging you, I'm not. My husband also lost a leg in Afghanistan."

The woman's eyes bulged. "And you cope with things okay?"

"We both do. He accepted the loss of his limb from the outset. Now and again, an infection flares up, but basically, he's no different to any other man I've come into contact with over the years. He's a very determined man, so I suppose I'm fortunate in that respect."

"Aren't you the lucky one? Rob used to wake me up screaming. I was constantly changing our sheets because of the sweat pouring out of him every night. I'm not a hard cow ordinarily, Inspector. However, when Rob refused to continue seeing his psychiatrist, I realised the writing was on the wall for us... and our marriage. I couldn't put my kids through the shouting and the trauma every day. It wasn't fair on them to witness his vast swings in behaviour. It confused the hell out of them to see their father like that."

"When he was seeing his psychiatrist, things were better between you?"

"I'd say they were manageable. His moods were monitored better. But recently, he said the voices had become louder, more insistent. Please, I need to know why you felt the need to come here with an armed response team. What has Rob done?"

Lorne inhaled a large breath. "Have you seen the local news lately, Mrs. Lawton?"

Her brow furrowed, and she scratched the side of her head. "Kind of. Some days, I do; others, I don't. What are you referring to?"

"The murders that have taken place at local cinemas?"

"I seem to remember vaguely hearing something about them. Why?"

Lorne's eyes fixed on the woman's, until the realisation dawned on her.

"No! You're not telling me that Rob is responsible for the murders?"

Lorne nodded. "We believe so. Not only in London but also in Manchester. Can you think of any reason why he would travel to Manchester?"

Mrs. Lawton contemplated the question for a few seconds then clicked her fingers. "His best mate used to live up there, before he was killed in action. He died in the same incident that injured Rob, actually."

"That explains it then. Do you know where your husband is staying now?"

"No, I have no idea. He refused to give me his address. I need to ask how you know that Rob is responsible for these crimes."

"His DNA and fingerprints were found in a house in Manchester, connected to a Ford Granada witnessed leaving the scene of a murder. We have a rape victim who was left at the side of the road on the M6, and she told us about the scarring to his face and identified his car. We have also matched Rob's DNA to the DNA recovered from the victim's body. A witness to one of the cinema murders saw his artificial leg. You see, it all adds up. Your husband does drive a black Ford Granada, right?"

Mrs. Lawton's head sank onto her chest. "Yes. I can't believe he would do such a thing. To rape and murder people! That's not the Rob I once knew and loved."

"I'm so sorry to break the news to you in this way. Now you can understand why I wanted the children out of the way before I spoke to you."

The woman gasped. "My God! What if he comes back here? Tries to kill us? Takes the kids from me, even?"

"He won't. I'll ensure that doesn't happen, if you're willing to help us."

"I can't believe you're trying to barter with me, or is this some kind of blackmail, Inspector? You'll help me only if I help you in return? What happens if I refuse? You'll cast us aside to deal with a madman?"

"That's not what I said. If it came across that way, then I'm really sorry."

"It did. I want police protection. I don't care what happens to me, but I will not put my kids' lives in danger."

"We can arrange that, although I don't perceive you to be in any danger, if I'm honest. If that was his intention, he would have come after you all by now."

"How did you figure that one out, Inspector? I lived with the man, for God's sake, and didn't have a clue what he was going to do next."

"Point taken. Is there a relative you can stay with, perhaps?"

"And put someone else's life in danger in the process? No!"

"I understand. Let me see if it's possible to get something organised for you tonight. Please, you've got to try and help us find your husband in return. If we can take him into custody, you'll be safe from harm."

"I don't know what else I can tell you. I have no idea where he's staying. I've had no direct contact with him in over a month. I'm at a loss, just like you are, apparently."

"Okay, let me make a few calls. In the meantime, do you want to start packing a few bags for yourself and the children? Do you have a car?"

"No. I rely on public transport to get me everywhere. I can't afford the upkeep of a car when Rob doesn't pay me any maintenance for the kids. I'll go and pack. Can I take the kids upstairs with me? There will be things they'll specifically want to take with them, and their favourite toys vary from week-to-week."

"Of course. Wait, can you tell me the registration number of Rob's car?"

"No. I've never taken much notice of that type of thing." She walked through the double doors to the dining room. "Sandy, Carl, we're going on a little adventure for a few days, and we need to pack a bag each. Do you want to help me choose what we take with us?"

"Are we going on holiday, Mummy?" the little girl asked.

"Sort of, sweetheart. Come on, we don't have much time."

After the family marched upstairs, Tony joined Lorne in the lounge. "What's going on? Don't tell me you've invited them to stay with us?"

Lorne tilted her head. "Are you objecting to that scenario, husband dearest?"

"Well..."

She punched him in the arm. "Don't worry, I did no such thing. I'm going to try and arrange temporary police protection for them until he's caught." She smiled at the relief on her husband's face then dialled the station, but unfortunately her call to the appropriate department went unanswered. "Damn, the office is shut until the morning. We're going to have to..."

Tony cringed. "Yes?"

"Take them to a hotel for now."

"Makes sense to me. They need to get out of here." Something caught Tony's eye through the lounge window. "What the fuck!"

"Oh, bugger. It's the media. How the heck did they find out?"

"Probably one of the neighbours rang them when the ART was raiding the joint. We definitely need to get the family away from here now, because if Lawton sees this on his TV screen tonight, there's no telling how he's going to react."

"Shit, you're right. I need to get out there and start issuing warnings to them. Maybe they'll take the hint and bugger off before they film the family leaving." She stormed out the house and marched over to the reporter and her cameraman. "Sorry, wasted trip, guys. There's nothing to see here."

"Ah, Inspector Warner, if there's nothing to see, then why are you here?"

"Visiting a friend." Lorne grinned broadly at the smartarse reporter, who was sporting a smug grin.

"Is that so? We have reason to believe that some form of hostage situation was taking place here."

Lorne let out a full belly laugh. "And how many hoax calls like that do you get a day, Maria?"

"Too many to mention. However, my interest piqued when I saw you emerge from the house."

"Like I said, I'm visiting a friend." Luckily, no cameras were rolling.

"You're telling me that an ART didn't turn up at this address?"

"Nope. Sorry. As previously stated, you've had a wasted trip, guys. Now toddle off home."

Just then, a man shouted behind Lorne. "Over here. This is what I saw. I'm the one who called you."

Lorne groaned and turned around to face the man. He was holding his mobile phone out to the reporter. She pondered confiscating the phone but couldn't come up with a reasonable excuse to get it out of the man's grubby little hands. Lorne flung her arms out to the side. "Bloody busybodies. I'm warning you guys—either you hold off filming until I get the family away from here, or I'll charge you with interfering with a police investigation. Is that clear?"

"We'll see what the old man has to show us first, Inspector."

Lorne caught the cocky reporter's arm and hitched it up. "No, you won't. You'll let me get the family to safety before you go near that gentleman. That's my final warning on the matter. Do you *understand* me?"

"Yes, okay. You win."

As Lorne stormed back to the house, she glanced sideways at the gentleman who was eager to have a word with the reporter, and shook her head in disgust. He had the decency to look embarrassed, but instead of retreating into his house, he veered off in the reporter's direction.

"Everything all right, Lorne?" Tony asked tentatively.

Seething, she hissed, "No, it's not. Let's hurry them up and get out of here."

Heroic Justice

The subdued family were ready to leave twenty minutes later. Tony had decided it would be better if he stayed outside the property in the car on surveillance for the night and had arranged for a taxi to pick up Lorne and the Lawtons.

"I'll be in touch later, love." Lorne pecked Tony on the lips after the family had been loaded into the taxi, then she jumped in the backseat herself. As they turned the corner, Lorne found it hard to suppress the sudden griping in her stomach, telling her that something terrible was about to happen either to her or to Tony. Trying to set her ominous feeling to one side, she asked Beth Lawton if Rob had any relatives in the area he might visit.

She shook her head. "No, he has a brother living in Manchester. That's all he has now. God, I should have thought of him earlier, sorry. Not that he's seen Malcolm in a while; he's a bit of a loner."

"Do you have any contact details for him?"

"No, sorry. It's Malcolm Lawton, and he lives in Didsbury, if that helps?"

Lorne jotted the name down in her notebook. "What about the army? Maybe I can have a chat with his commanding officer, see what he can tell me about Rob."

"Colonel Drake is the person you need to contact. He's also based in Manchester."

"Did you live in Manchester at one time?"

Beth nodded. "For a few months, in temporary army housing, until we decided to buy our own house. I wanted to move down here to be closer to my family. Rob didn't object at the time, but the cost of living in London is exorbitant compared to Manchester, and it soon became a problem between us."

"I see... well, this is all starting to add up now. Why he travelled to Manchester to..." Lorne cut the sentence there, aware the kids were listening to their conversation. She saw Beth exhale a relieved sigh. "What regiment was Rob in?"

"The Duke of Lancaster Regiment."

Lorne jotted down the information as the taxi driver drew up outside a small bed-and-breakfast in a quaint tree-lined street. "Here we are. I've got your number, and I should get back to you tomorrow with something a little more permanent for you all. I'll help you in with your bags."

"Thank you, that's very kind of you."

"Can you wait for me?" Lorne asked the driver. "I'll need a lift home."

The man nodded but remained in his cab instead of helping them with the bags.

"The meter is running," he grumbled as Lorne got out of the car.

She rang the bell, and a brunette lady wearing a colourful dress and a friendly smile welcomed them into the hallway. "Hello there. I've put you in the family room at the back of the house. It's quieter there away from the main road, not that it ever gets really noisy."

"Wonderful, thank you," Beth said, sounding grateful, as the five of them climbed the stairs with the luggage.

Lorne cast her eyes around the room, and satisfied that she'd made the right choice for the family, she left them to it. "I'll call you tomorrow. Sleep well."

"Thank you, Inspector," Beth replied with watery eyes.

Once she was back in the taxi, Lorne gave her address to the driver and rested her head against the headrest. It had been a long day. Her thoughts lay with her husband, who was having to stay awake all night in case Lawton turned up at his home. She felt relieved, though, that they'd managed to get the family away from the area before the reporter began her bulletin. As soon as she arrived at the house, Lorne switched on the TV and put on the news. She shook her head when she saw Maria's broadcast being aired. *I wonder how Rob is going to react when he sees his house on TV.*

CHAPTER NINETEEN

Lorne hardly slept that night. She felt strange not having Tony lying in the bed next to her. They'd barely been apart since tying the knot.

In the morning, the phone rang at seven as she was preparing breakfast for Charlie and herself. "Hi, love. I take it Lawton didn't turn up overnight?"

"Nope, it was a waste of time. I half expected him to show up after that idiot did her broadcast."

"Me, too. I watched it and cringed. If Lawton did see it, I reckon he would have been incensed."

"Enough for him to go on the rampage again and choose yet another victim?"

"And some. I'm just heading off for work now—thought I'd go in early as I haven't slept much."

"Nice to hear that you missed me."

"Did I say that? Sheba kept me company all night."

"I knew you'd be too scared to sleep alone. I'm coming home now. I'll see you later. Give me a ring if you need a hand with anything during the day."

"I will, and, Tony... thank you for going the extra mile on this one. Not sure what I'd do without you."

"You're welcome. Speak later."

Lorne hung up, grabbed a piece of toast, kissed Charlie on the forehead, and ran out the back door. "Have a good day, love."

Charlie waved her off. "Take care out there, Mum."

"I will. Likewise around here, sweetie."

Lorne met Katy in the station car park. "You look how I feel, love. Bad night again?"

"Yep. Why do you look rough?"

"I'll fill you in over coffee."

The rest of the team reported for work early as promised, so Lorne relayed the events of what had happened the previous evening.

"Tony stayed there all night?" Katy asked in disbelief.

Lorne shrugged. "It was his choice. My main concern was getting the family into digs and away from the house ASAP."

"Where do we go from here?"

"I have a couple of perspectives that I need to look into. Rob's brother, Malcolm, and his commanding officer, Colonel Drake."

Katy nodded. "Want me to take the brother?"

"That'd be great. Just make general enquiries as to when he saw him last, that sort of thing, and we'll go from there. I'll be in my office, trying to make contact with the colonel. The rest of you just keep digging, check to see if anyone has reported either spotting Lawton's car or him. We'll share what we find in half an hour or so." She stopped at the coffee machine before she entered the office, pausing to inhale her morning reminder of Pete.

A few sips of coffee later, Lorne rang the number she had looked up for The Duke of Lancaster regiment. She was patched through to three different departments before an abrupt voice answered her call. "Colonel Drake, who is this?"

"Good morning, Colonel. Sorry to ring you so early. I'm DI Lorne Warner of the Metropolitan Police in London. Do you have a moment?"

"Met Police? In regard to what, Inspector?"

"Robert Lawton, a soldier who used to serve under you."

"Ah, yes," he said, his voice softening. "He used to be a good soldier."

"Used to be? Meaning what?"

"Between you and me, I feel the army let him down badly."

"In what respect? By dismissing him?"

"Yes. He served his country well. He lost several dear friends and comrades in the attack."

"I heard. Is that when his PTSD commenced?"

"I believe so. He was badly injured and spent a couple of months in hospital. Used to wake up screaming in the middle of the night, so the nurses told me. Terrible situation. He's not alone, either. Unfortunately, hundreds of men return from serving in the battlefield and struggle to settle back into civilian life."

"Can I ask if you've heard from him lately?"

"No... what's this really about, Inspector?"

Lorne sighed and leaned back in her chair. "Have you seen the news recently?"

Heroic Justice

"Yes, anything in particular you're referring to?"

"The murders that have taken place in cinemas in London and in Manchester—we're treating Rob as our main suspect."

The colonel gasped. "You're kidding me?"

"I'm afraid not. Rob's wife hasn't been in contact with him in quite some time, and he hasn't been living at his address. Is there anything you can tell me about Rob that might hint at where he could be right now?"

Lorne's question was met with a few moments' silence. "I have no idea... I'm sorry, but this whole conversation has left me bewildered, Inspector. You think he's murdered several people, and you have no idea where he is?"

"No. He's moved between London and Manchester at least twice, and he doesn't seem to be in contact with his family or former friends."

"Was his wife not worried that he'd been gone so long?"

"They're currently separated. I've taken the precaution of putting his wife and children in a safe house."

"Oh my. I just don't know what to say, Inspector. The man's personality altered dramatically a few months after he was injured, and instead of the army standing by him, they washed their hands of him. That truly stuck in my throat. But my Brigadier made the decision to set him loose. To me, it's like arming him with an AK-47 and placing him in a school playground, and from what you've just told me, that impression isn't too far off the mark."

"It's sickening. I thought the army always did their best to support the soldiers who have served under them, but I guess I was wrong about that."

"Ninety-nine percent of the time, I would say that's true, Inspector," the colonel countered.

"Oh well, if you can't steer me in any kind of direction, I suppose I better get on. Thank you for speaking to me."

"Anytime. I'm always there for my men, if they need any help, whether they are still serving under me or not. I hope you find him before he takes another victim. Ring me if you need anything further."

"Thank you, I will." Lorne hung up, leaned back in her chair, and exhaled, puffing out her cheeks.

Katy appeared in the doorway, her eyes wide and her cheeks pale.

Lorne bounced upright. "I'm not going to like this, am I?"

"It may not be connected. It's probably me jumping the gun, but..."

"Come on, Katy, out with it."

"There's been a report of another hitchhiker being attacked on the M6."

"Shit! Do we have any witnesses?"

"Yes, an elderly man said he saw a white van speeding away from a lay-by. The van almost took his front bumper off. He thought it looked suspicious, so he pulled over, and that's when he found the half-dressed woman. He called an ambulance and the police right away."

"What about the woman? Did she make it?"

"Yes, she's in the hospital, Birmingham Hospital."

"Did the witness get a registration number on the van?"

Katy shook her head. "Unfortunately, no. It has to be him, though, right? He's swapped vehicles on us."

"I think you're right, Katy. It was only a matter of time before he went down that route. Perhaps he senses that we're closing the net in on him."

Katy snorted. "If only that was true. What's our next step?"

"Get me the proper location of where the incident took place. We need to visit the girl in hospital to verify that it was Lawton who attacked her. Once we know that, I'd like Graham to start ringing around all the second-hand garages in the London area to find Lawton's Granada."

"That could take days, Lorne."

She shrugged. "I'm open to suggestions as to how we're supposed to locate his vehicle, Katy. Feel free to chip in at any time."

Katy's mouth gaped open.

"I'm sorry, I really didn't mean to snap. It's just so exasperating the way he's tying us in knots at the moment. Let me ring DI Nelson, make him aware of what could be heading his way."

Katy left the room. Lorne picked up her phone and dialled Hero's number. "Hi, Hero. It's Lorne Warner."

"Lorne, I was just thinking about ringing you. Have you got some news for me?"

"I might have. I need to visit someone in hospital first. Here's what we're looking at..." She recapped what Katy had just told her and sighed.

"I think you could be right. Any suggestions what we do next?"

"I thought I'd drop in and see the girl then make my way up there. He's obviously heading in your direction. I could fill you in on what else has been going on while I'm there."

"Sounds brilliant. Will Tony be coming with you?"

"I think I'd have a devil of a job stopping him. I'll ring him now and get back to you when I've firmed up my plans. I'll have to run it past my DCI of course, too."

"You do that. In the meantime, I'll put an alert out for the van. Don't hold out much hope of getting anywhere with that, though, not without having a reg number to go on."

"Every little bit helps at this stage. Speak soon." Lorne debated a few seconds whether she should get Tony involved, but she quickly realised he would be livid with her if she didn't at least call to tell him what was happening.

She cringed when his groggy voice answered the phone. "Love, I'm so sorry to disturb your sleep. But I thought you'd want to be involved."

"I'm awake now. What is it, Lorne? Have you spotted Lawton?"

"I have a woman in hospital, another hitchhiker on the road to Manchester. I'm going to travel up there and continue on to Manchester if her attacker's description matches Lawton. I wondered if you wanted to come along for the ride."

"It's a no-brainer, love. I'll pack an overnight bag for us both on the proviso that you don't have a go at me if I forget something."

She laughed. "I promise. Can you be here within the hour?"

"How about forty-five minutes?"

"Perfect. See you soon. I'll drive."

"Might be a good idea, given how much sleep I've had."

Lorne ignored the morning post sitting in her in-tray and walked out of the office to bring the team up to date. "Katy, I'm going to set off soon, and Tony is on his way, as he'll be joining me. You're going to have to hold the fort here, if that's all right?"

"Sure. I think you're doing the right thing."

Lorne nodded then clicked her fingers. "Damn, I forgot the most important thing I had to do this morning. We need to get onto Witness Protection, sort out some kind of accommodation for the Lawton family. Can you do that for me?"

"Leave it with me."

"Great." She turned to Graham. "I know I may be jumping the gun a little, but my gut says this guy is behind this attack, so I would like you to ring every second-hand garage in the London area and see if you can find Lawton's Granada. Maybe he traded the Granada in."

"What if I check to see if a white van has been reported stolen? That should cover all the options, boss."

"Good thinking. We need that registration number ASAP."

Graham gave her an enthusiastic nod. "Yes, boss."

"And, Karen, can you track down a Malcolm Lawton in the Didsbury area of Manchester for me? He's Rob's brother, so play it cautiously. Just enquire if he's seen him recently and ask him to ring us if Rob does make contact with him."

"Will do, boss."

"Right, I better go and run all this past the DCI, so wish me luck."

Lorne walked along the corridor to Roberts's office. Roberts seemed pleased to see her for a change—that was, until she explained why she'd come.

"Am I to understand that you're deserting your post yet again, Inspector?"

"Hardly, sir. Needs must if we want to catch this bastard."

"I'm jesting. Of course you have my backing, as long as Katy is all right to fill in for you."

"She appreciates the magnitude of the situation, Sean. I have a good feeling about this trip. His family is safe and out of harm's way, so that's a load off my mind. Umm... I forgot to mention that Tony will be going with me. Is that okay with you?"

"Good. Actually, I was about to suggest the same. Either that, or I postpone my meeting with the superintendent and accompany you myself."

Lorne cringed. "That would have been... umm... nice."

"You're a dreadful liar, Lorne Warner. Now go catch me a killer."

She stood up as her face flushed. "I'll do my very best. Thanks, Sean. I'll keep you updated."

"Make sure you do. Good luck with your manhunt."

"I'll be taking my Taser with me, just in case. Shame I'm not authorised to carry a real gun."

"Don't start, Lorne. It is what it is. At least you're Taser-trained now, and that's a step in the right direction."

Heroic Justice

"Hmm... okay. I'll be in touch soon." I still reckon it's going to take more than a Taser to bring this guy down!

CHAPTER TWENTY

When Tony arrived at the station, the desk sergeant called Lorne's office.

After saying her farewells to the team, she raced down the stairs to meet her husband. "Hello, you. Sorry you didn't get much sleep." She kissed Tony on the cheek, and they rushed out to the car.

"No problem. Maybe I can have a snooze en route. Are you sure this isn't going to be a wild-goose chase?"

"Nope. But I feel it's the right thing to do at this point. Let's see what the woman in hospital has to say first. We can always turn back if she indicates we're on the wrong track."

Just over two hours and twenty minutes later, Lorne was standing alongside the battered woman's bedside while Tony waited in the hall with a uniformed officer. Dee Williams had been conscious for less than a couple of hours and was still very woozy. Her head was bandaged, she had two black eyes from the broken nose she'd suffered, and her right shoulder had been dislocated.

"Hello, Dee. How are you feeling?"

Her head dipped onto her chest, and she looked embarrassed. "Very sore and rather foolish to have accepted a lift."

"You're not the first, and I doubt you'll be the last, to say that, hon. Can you tell me what the man looked like? Any distinguishing features, perhaps? His hair colour, height and build?"

"His hair was light brown. Average weight, I suppose, but I couldn't tell his height because he was sitting down." She paused, and her eyes narrowed as she recalled the next piece of information. "I didn't notice it at first. He didn't look at me when he pulled over, but during the journey, he glanced my way and... well... his face was..." She covered her face with her hands. "I know I shouldn't have, but I screeched when I saw the horrific scars on his face. Do you think that's why he attacked me?"

"I doubt it, love. This man has been on our radar for a few weeks now. The crimes he's committed have no reasoning behind them."

She looked up at Lorne and frowned. "I don't understand. You mean he's intentionally targeting hitchhikers? I've been doing it for years and never once had a problem, until now."

"He's only recently begun to target hitchhikers. We weren't sure that the previous victim wasn't an isolated incident, but we did issue a warning on the news last week. Did you not see it?"

"No, I've been travelling for weeks, staying in hostels, and I haven't seen any television in that time."

"I see. This man, did he strike up a conversation with you about where he was going? Anything like that?"

"No. Nothing. There was an awkward silence in the vehicle. I've never had that before. I felt uncomfortable the second I hopped into the van. I wish I'd had the balls to jump out, but he was doing eighty on the motorway."

"Would you mind making an official statement for us? The sooner, the better. Has anyone from the hospital contacted your relatives?"

"Yes, my mum and dad are on their way to collect me. They'll be here in a few hours. They're coming up from Essex."

"I can get the officer outside to take your statement, if that's all right?"

"I can do my best." Her hand touched her bandaged head. "It's all still a little fuzzy, and I want to be as accurate as I can for you."

"Just tell the officer what you've told me already. You've done so well. I really appreciate that. Have they carried out the tests? To obtain any DNA?"

"Yes. I said I wanted it done as soon as I woke up."

Lorne nodded and smiled.

"The doctor said I should be released tomorrow, providing my recovery goes well."

Lorne patted her on the hand. "I need to shoot off now. Thank you so much for your help, and I'll leave you to rest. Glad you're still here. Just be careful about hitching a ride in the future."

"No more hitching for me, I can assure you. I hope you catch him. I want my day in court facing the..."

"You'll get it. Don't worry. Take care of yourself."

Lorne collected Tony and returned to the car. En route to Manchester, she rang Katy and confirmed that Dee Williams's description of her attacker matched Rob Lawton. Then she rang Hero and advised him that Robert Lawton was likely in his area.

"Thanks for that, Lorne. I'm going to call another press conference. Let's try and flush the bugger out. I'm going to name him, if that's all right with you?"

"Perfect. Do me a favour and mention his scarred face and that he has an artificial leg. People should be made aware of that. We need to find him quickly—he's becoming more erratic. I'm wondering—I've seen it before with other criminals—if he's building up to his endgame. We need to put both forces on high alert. Get the patrol vehicles to check every white van they come across, if that's possible. Every copper on the force should be keeping their eyes peeled for Robert Lawton."

"You're right. I'll get my team to start spreading the word now, Lorne. I'll see you in a few hours."

"Good luck with the press conference. Don't hold back. Let's meet fire with fire on this one."

~ ~ ~

Hero greeted Lorne and Tony with an unexpected hug when they arrived at the station a few hours later.

"Lovely to meet you again, Patch, even if it is under dire circumstances. We heard the news conference on the radio," Tony said.

"And?" he asked, his eyes wide with expectation.

"You nailed it. Said all the things I would have told the listening public. If that doesn't get the calls flooding in, nothing will. Any chance of a coffee around here?" Lorne asked with a wink.

Hero ushered them both into his office and asked Julie to join them and to bring four cups of coffee with her.

With everyone assembled in the medium-sized room, they hatched a plan on what to do next. "Of course, it's going to depend on what information the public feeds us," Lorne began, "but my take is that we action every call as it comes in. As soon as there is a lead, we pounce."

"What if that lead turns out to be a duff one?" Julie mumbled.

"Julie's right," Hero agreed. "You know as well as I do how these things usually pan out, Lorne. We're bound to get the odd screwball ringing up to try and put us off the scent."

"I know. All right, how about we all take a vote on the information? I know I work a lot on gut feelings. Not sure if that works for you guys? However, between us, we should get an inkling if the information is legit or not, right?"

Julie shrugged, and Hero nodded. "Okay, that's a deal," he said.

"Let's hope the phone starts ringing soon," Tony said.

"I was just thinking the same," Lorne agreed. She almost jumped out of her skin when her mobile rang. "Hi, Katy, we've arrived. What have you got?"

"Glad to hear it. Graham struck gold. He's found the garage who swapped the Granada for a van. Do you want the reg?"

Lorne withdrew her notebook and pen and jotted down the information. "Give Graham a pat on the back from me, tell him I owe him a pint. I'm probably telling you how to suck eggs, but contact SOCO and get them to look over the car."

"Already done. I'm about to go out and collect the family, to transport them to a safe house. That should put your mind at ease on that front."

"Phew! That is a relief. Thanks for that, Katy. Guard that address with your life, as we'll treat it on a need-to-know basis."

"Will do. I hope your visit north does the trick. I caught the news in my break. That Hero Nelson is a sexy bugger. I can understand why you were eager to go up there."

Lorne felt the colour rise in her cheeks. She didn't have the balls to look in either Hero's or Tony's direction. "Thanks for that, Katy. Tony sends his love."

Katy's laughter filled her ear before she ended the call.

Lorne cleared her throat. "We've got the van's reg. Can you distribute that to the patrols on the street?" Lorne slid the details across the desk to Hero. "Katy also said that the Lawtons are on their way to a safe house, or they will be soon. So that's one less thing we have to worry about."

"Brilliant news on both counts. Julie, can you get this actioned ASAP?" Hero passed the van details to his partner, who was already on her feet and ready to sprint out the door.

When Julie left the office, Lorne heard several phones ringing.

"I think we're in the wrong office, don't you?" Hero asked.

Lorne lifted her cup and nodded. "Yep, I'm with you on that one."

The three of them circulated the incident room, sifting through the information that was coming in. Their newfound insight into the way the killer's mind worked made that task much easier.

Lorne struck upon a report of a sighting in Salford Quays. "Hero, over here. What do you think of this?" She handed Hero the note as he approached.

"Hmm... I could get uniform to take a look."

"Do that."

Hero actioned the task immediately as yet more information arrived. Before long, they were drowning in well-meant data.

"Agh... best-laid plans," Lorne grumbled. "Why is it we rarely get a response like this in our neck of the woods?"

"I did think your idea about pouncing on the info as it came in was a little beyond our realms, shall I say?" Hero chuckled.

"You should have reined me in."

"I hate to dampen anyone's enthusiasm, especially someone as senior as you, Lorne."

~ ~ ~

The rest of the afternoon left them reeling. Checking through all the information they had gathered left them a little bewildered. Reports from the public placed Lawton in all four corners of Manchester within half an hour.

"Bloody hell, that's really disheartening," Lorne said, thumping her clenched fist against her thigh.

All their irritation dissipated when they received a call from the control room telling them that a patrol car had located the van a few streets away from the station. Lorne's eyes narrowed at the news.

Tony nudged her. "What are you thinking?"

"That he's up to something. Why so close to the station?" Lorne replied in a hushed voice.

Just then, Hero received a text, and when he looked up from his phone, all the colour had drained from his face. His shoulders slumped as he fell into the chair next to him.

"Crap, Patch, what's wrong?" Lorne asked.

He handed her his phone.

Heroic Justice

She read the message aloud so Tony could hear. "'I have your sister. Do what I ask and she won't get hurt. If you refuse...'" She looked up at Hero and asked, "What if this is another prank?"

Hero shook his head and exhaled deeply. "That text was sent from Cara's phone."

"Shit! I'm so sorry, Hero. We'll do as he says. We need to think positive at all times."

"You don't understand, Lorne, Cara is in a bad place right now. We've just lost our father; this is the last thing she needs. Damn, she only came back to work on Monday."

"I do understand. I remember you telling me that your father had recently died. Come on, between us, we've got this covered."

Hero looked around the room at his team. Everyone had stopped answering the phones and was just staring at him.

Lorne clapped to get their attention. "Guys, come on. We're better than him. Remember that. Do *not* let him sense he has one over on us."

"But he has," Hero mumbled.

Lorne shook his shoulders. "No, he hasn't. Text him back, ask him what he wants in return for Cara's safety. Come on, Patch, hold it together, for your family's sake."

"How did you cope? When that crazy bastard kidnapped Charlie?"

"I dug deep. I knew Charlie wouldn't want me to crumble, and she was expecting me to rescue her." She turned to Tony and held out her hand for him to take. "I couldn't have done that without Tony's help." She faced Hero again. "You have the A-Team working alongside you on this one, love. We'll get her back, I promise you. Just trust us."

"Can you text him back? I think my hands are shaking too much."

Lorne nodded. "What shall we say?"

"My head isn't clear enough to think. It's your call."

She punched in a message then tilted the phone in his direction. "How's that? It's brief and to the point." The message read: *You have my attention. I'm willing to give you what you want.*

Hero nodded. "Send it."

Lorne hit the send button, then they all paced the floor for the next fifteen minutes until the reply tinkled on Hero's phone. Standing side-by-side, Lorne and Hero read the message together.

I want my wife and children here. NOW.

"Shit!" Lorne shot Tony a worried glance.

"What does it say?" Tony demanded.

Lorne held out the phone for him to read himself. "Oh, crap! You can't let that happen."

Hero's eyes widened. "You know what the consequences are if we don't comply with his wishes, man."

"I know, but there has to be a way around this," Tony said, sinking onto the desk behind him.

Another text message from Cara's phone arrived. *Why the delay? Do I have to hurt your sister?*

"Please, we have to think of something to say to keep him from doing that," Hero pleaded.

Lorne typed a message back: *We're trying to contact your wife now.* "That should appease him for now. In the meantime, we need to consider the consequences if we bring his wife and children up here."

"If we don't, he's going to kill Cara, and I can't allow that to happen."

Tony nodded. "Hero is right, Lorne. We need to bring them up here. Once we have a meeting place agreed, we'll sort out a plan to swoop on Lawton and get Cara. I'll do it, if I have to."

"You can't, Tony. Not with your leg."

He waved away her concerns. "It's fine. What's an artificial leg amongst friends when there are lives at stake?"

"It's your call, Lorne," Hero prompted.

Lorne swept a hand over her cheeks. "Shit. Roberts is going to have my head on a plate for this. Okay, let's do it. I just hope the wife will oblige us in our decision."

"Use my office to make the call," Hero suggested, looking more relieved than he had a few seconds before.

On heavy legs, Lorne marched into Hero's office and placed the call to Beth Lawton. "Hello, Beth. It's DI Lorne Warner."

"Hello, Inspector. Thank you ever so much for arranging this house for us. We've settled in really quickly."

Lorne closed her eyes, hating herself for what she was about to ask of this family.

"I'm glad to hear it... but, Beth, I have a favour to ask."

"Go on."

Lorne could hear the hesitancy in her voice. "Rob has made contact with us. I'm in Manchester at present."

"Right. Why are you telling me this?"

Lorne gulped noisily. "Well, he has taken a hostage. We're closing in on him, but he's just pulled the rug from underneath us, and we need your help to put things right."

"What? My help? He won't listen to me, Inspector."

"I think he might. He said he wants to see you."

"I can't. I don't think I could face him again knowing what he's done."

"I know, and I completely understand how you must feel, but he has a hostage, and all I'm trying to do is save her life."

"By jeopardising mine?"

"No. I would *never* put your life in jeopardy. There would be dozens of police officers there, and as soon as the opportunity arises, we'll make our move and overpower him."

"What? You want to use me as bait?"

Lorne cringed. Beth had hit the nail on the head. "Yes and no. We wouldn't let him get near you or the children, I swear."

"What? You never mentioned the children. I won't do it, Inspector. I would never endanger my children's lives in this way. Goodbye."

Beth hung up, and Lorne placed her head in her hands. She detested being placed in the middle like this. She heard a knock on the door, and she pulled her hands away from her face to find Tony rushing towards her.

"I'm all right," she said. "Just pissed off. I couldn't persuade her. I did my best, but looking at it from her angle, I probably would have done the same to protect my children."

"Okay. Come on, Lorne, don't give up at the first sign of trouble. We'll find a way of getting around this. Have faith."

Hero walked into the room. "I take it that the call didn't go down too well with the wife?"

"It was to be expected. We're not going to give up, Patch. We'll lie to him if we have to."

"You mean pretend the wife has agreed to the meeting?"

"Yes. Then we show up in force and arrest him."

He sank into a chair. "If only things were that simple. You know how handy this madman is with a knife. What if he slices my sister's throat in the process? I could never forgive myself if that happens, Lorne. Can't we force the wife to come up here?"

"Now you're just talking nonsense. Put yourself in the woman's shoes, Hero. How would you feel if this was being asked of Fay and the kids?"

His head bowed. "I know. I'm sorry, but Cara is all over the place at present. If it wasn't for Dad's passing, she would kick the shit out of him, and the guy wouldn't stand a chance. Her combined police and TA training would be no match for an injured army man, I can assure you."

"Maybe you're doing your sister an injustice, Hero. Perhaps she's thinking up a plan of her own right now of how she can overpower him. I say we text Lawton back and tell him we agree to the exchange."

"And when we turn up there and he sees no sign of his wife and kids? He'll react quickly, know that we're trying to trap him."

Lorne's mobile rang, interrupting the conversation. Seeing it was Beth Lawton calling, Lorne scrambled to answer it. "Hello, Beth. Everything all right?"

"I'll do it. I couldn't live with the guilt of knowing I could have prevented him from taking another life. On one proviso."

Lorne gave Tony and Hero the thumbs-up. "What's that, love?"

"The first sign of trouble, and you take him out. Whether it puts the hostage's life in danger or not. I need to protect myself and my kids at all costs."

"I couldn't agree more. Beth, we can't thank you enough for this. I'll get in touch with Katy and arrange for your transportation up here. Don't worry, we have super-experienced people watching your back on this one. I promise you."

"That's good to hear. I feel I owe you for coming to our rescue, Inspector. I'll wait to hear from your colleague."

"I can't thank you enough. She shouldn't be long, I promise." Lorne disconnected the call and high-fived Hero and Tony. "Whatever we do, we need to ensure that family's safety. Deal?"

Hero nodded emphatically. "Damn right that's a deal." Then he let out a relieved sigh.

"I need to ring Katy now."

Tony and Hero left the office again, giving her the privacy needed to make the call.

Heroic Justice

"Katy, we've made a deal with the devil. I need either you or a member of the team, to pick up Beth Lawton and her kids and bring them up to Manchester."

"What the fu...? You've lost your mind. May I ask why?"

Lorne explained the situation about the proposed swap with Hero's sister.

"I repeat, you've lost your mind this time, Lorne."

"Hey, thanks for the vote of confidence, mate. We've got it covered. Don't forget we have Tony's covert expertise available, and Hero is also ex-TA, and with my negotiating skills, we've got every angle covered. We're wasting time, Katy. Beth has agreed to trust us, and that's all that matters, right? We're not about to put their lives in danger."

"Whatever. Right, I'm going to bring them up myself. I need to see how this pans out first hand."

Lorne laughed. "I knew you wouldn't be able to resist the temptation to get involved."

"You know me better than I know myself. I'll see you in three or four hours, depending on the traffic."

"Drive carefully, hon." Lorne joined the others in the incident room and took Hero aside. "One question has been bugging me."

"And that is?"

"How did he get hold of Cara? How did he know who she was?"

"In case you hadn't realised, those were two questions you just asked."

Lorne pulled a face at him.

"Seriously, though, I was wondering the same. Maybe I pissed him off during the TV appeal and he Googled me. It wouldn't be hard to put two and two together and come up with Cara's name. She's my twin, and we've followed the same path a few times. She was in the TA with me, as well."

"Hmm... I suspect you're right. So, that means Cara will likely help us in any rescue attempt. She's not a girly girl, I take it?"

"Your assumption is spot-on. She has her moments at being girly, but when the need arises, she could give any of her TA colleagues a run for their money. She's kicked my arse a few times in the past, I can tell you. It's just... well, I'm concerned by her current state of mind." He blew out an exasperated breath.

Lorne rubbed his arm. "Hey, if she's anything like you, I know when it comes to the crunch, she'll put up a good fight if necessary."

"Let's hope so. Are you going to send him another text?"

"Yep. Shall I agree to meet in five hours from now?"

Hero looked at the clock on the wall. "That's going to make it about eight o'clock. Do you think he'll go for that?"

"We won't give him the option. The night will be drawing in then and could work in our favour. Let's do this." Lorne typed into Hero's phone: *Your wife and children will be here within the next few hours. I think we should rendezvous at eight. Is that agreeable to you?*

No sooner had Lorne sent the message than the reply came through: *Eight is fine. Location—under the bridge on the canal path at Deansgate's Junction and Whitworth Road.*

Right away, the team set about organising plenty of backup to attend the scene. Then Katy and the Lawton family arrived a few minutes after seven. Lorne was relieved to see them all and smiled when they joined them for coffee and a sandwich. Not that anyone had much of an appetite.

At seven forty-five, the team left the station and made their way over to the rendezvous point.

"This is it!" Lorne reached for Tony's and Katy's hands. "Make or break time, kids."

"If we stick to the plan, everyone should pull through this safely," Tony reassured her.

Despite his words, Lorne had trouble dismissing the niggle of doubt gnawing away at her insides.

CHAPTER TWENTY-ONE

Lorne was just getting out of the car at the rendezvous point when her mobile rang, striking the fear of God into her. "Carol? Is everything all right?"

"I'm not sure, Lorne. I mean, all is well here, but I just had to ring you. The spirits are urging me to ring you to tell you to be careful. This man is extremely dangerous. It's the voices guiding every move he makes."

"I'll be careful, love. I appreciate the warning. Don't worry. We have things covered at this end."

"I know. Just be extra cautious. He's unpredictable. Bear that in mind, will you. Stay safe, darling."

"We all will, at least that's the plan. Thanks, Carol. I'll speak to' you soon." Lorne hung up and spotted Colonel Drake getting out of his car behind her. She rushed over to speak to him. "I hope you don't mind me calling you, sir? I just thought if he saw you here with us he may reconsider his actions."

"Let's hope so. Have you got plenty of police around, just in case things go wrong?"

Lorne nodded. "We're surrounded by officers. He won't be leaving the scene, whatever happens."

"Okay, let's ensure no further blood is lost, either his or the hostage. I see Beth and the kids are here. I'm sure that will mess with his mind, let's hope it's in a good way and he backs down after finally realising the devastation he's caused."

"That's what I'm hoping for. I need to organise my immediate team. Will you excuse me for a moment? I'll give you the nod if I need you."

"Of course. I'll be waiting for further instructions."

Lorne joined Hero, Tony and Katy to go over the final details of the plan. "I'm surprised he's not here yet. Do you think something has spooked him?"

Hero glanced at his watch. "He still has five minutes. So, Katy, you'll remain with Beth and the kids. Whatever happens, don't let them out of your sight."

Katy nodded. "I won't. We'll stay well back."

"Tony, you should go and get into position before Lawton shows up." Lorne kissed her husband on the cheek.

"Good luck, guys. We can do this," Tony said, holding up a clenched fist before he left the group.

Lorne watched him stride away from her, Carol's words of warning reverberating in her head.

Katy pointed at the tunnel. "Everything else will need to wait. He's arrived."

They watched Lawton emerge from the tunnel. He was holding a knife to Cara's throat. She looked understandably petrified. Lawton paused at the mouth of the tunnel. Hero went to step forward, but Lorne grabbed his arm. "Keep your temper in check, Patch. He won't do anything to mess things up. Katy, you better go back to Beth and the kids. Get them out of the car so he can see them, but don't bring them any closer."

"Going now. Good luck, guys." Katy rushed back to the car and asked the family to step out of the vehicle.

Sandy saw her father and immediately cried out to him. "Daddy! I love you, Daddy."

The innocent display of raw emotion made Lorne's eyes water. She studied Lawton's reaction. He strained his neck to see his daughter, but his grip on Cara's arm and the knife angled against her neck didn't falter.

"Here we go, Hero. Stay strong. We won't let anything happen to Cara, okay?"

"Let's hope not. I'm ready."

Lorne and Hero took a few steps closer to Lawton. "Stay there, or I'll hurt her."

They halted.

"There's no need for that, Rob," Lorne said, keeping her tone light and friendly. "We've done as instructed. Brought your family to see you. Why don't you let Cara go now?"

Lawton tipped back his head and roared with laughter. "What kind of fool do you think I am? I want my kids to come to me. Beth prevented me from seeing them, told me I had lost my mind and couldn't be trusted around them anymore. I bet she didn't tell you that, did she?"

Lorne's heart sank. "Rob, we can get you the help you need. Don't make this worse than it needs to be. Hand Cara over."

"She's my ticket out of here, Inspector. Stop treating me like an imbecile."

"You're not a fool, Rob, and I've never taken you for one. You've been to hell and back—I understand that. But we're all willing to help you now, to make amends for those who have failed you in the past. Even Colonel Drake is eager to help you." Lorne looked over her shoulder and beckoned him closer, but raised her hand to prevent him from coming too close.

"Hello, Rob. It's good to see you, mate. Why don't you let the girl go, and we'll sit down over a pint and discuss what help we can get you, eh?"

"They thought they'd bring you here to talk me around, but they were wrong. You let me down when I needed you the most. I gave my life to the army, and how did they repay me? By ditching me. Yes, I had a payoff, but it would never be enough, not for what the army took from me. I can't even bear to look at myself in the mirror now. Even my kids are scared of me. Nothing can compensate for that trauma."

"I'll fight your case through the courts to get you more compensation, Rob," Colonel Drake shouted.

"Ha, you're not listening to me, as usual, Colonel. It's not about the money. I'm half the man I used to be. My wife, who made an oath to love me through sickness and health, kicked me out of my own home when the going got tough. Everyone turned their back on me when all I needed was help to keep..."

"To keep what, Rob? The voices at bay?" Lorne said in a hushed voice.

He glared at her through narrowed eyes and remained silent for a moment. Lorne wondered if he was having an internal conversation with the voices ruling his head. Her heart went out to the man, in spite of how many innocent people he'd killed in the last few weeks. No one could really understand the trauma he was dealing with. "Rob, let us help you. We understand what you're going through. Let us be the ones to help you."

He shook his head violently and stared at Lorne. "No one can help me. I'm beyond help now."

Lorne saw something move above him, but she kept her eyes firmly focused on Lawton. "At least let us try, Rob. I've personally never let anyone down before. Give me the chance to make things right. Maybe even try and get you back with your family."

Lawton stared past her towards his family. Lorne nodded, and within seconds, Tony jumped from the bridge above and brought Lawton and Cara crashing to the ground. Lorne called out her husband's name as Hero rushed in to save his sister, pulling her away from Lawton's grip. Tony was writhing in agony a few feet behind Lawton. His artificial leg was lying a few feet away from him. Lawton jumped to his feet and looked down at the limb, confused. He tapped his own leg to see if it was still intact, and it was.

Lorne knew she had to draw his attention as she saw Lawton reach for something in his jacket. "Rob, we have Cara. Now it's time for you to tell us exactly what you need."

He slowly turned to face her. His hand came up to his head, and Lorne noticed that he was holding a hand-gun to his temple. His children and wife screamed.

"I'm no good to anyone. There truly is no hope for me in this world. I'm sorry, Beth, Sandy and Carl. I never stopped loving you. I hope you can forgive me for what I've done. I didn't mean to kill those people. *They* made me do it. No one knows what it's like to have a dozen or more voices nattering in your head. When I lie down at night to sleep, the voices goad me, they tell me how useless I am, force me to do things I just don't want to do."

"Give me the opportunity to help you, Rob. Please, don't do anything drastic. There are ways around this, I promise you." A lump developed in Lorne's throat as she felt a sudden bout of sympathy for the man.

"Will it give me my family back? Look at them—they're scared shitless of me. Why the fuck did I even join the army? They've done this to me. I never heard voices before I went out there, to Afghanistan. If it's not the voices destroying my mind, it's the explosions I constantly hear. Have you any idea what it's like to hear a full war zone playing out in your mind, hour after hour? I haven't slept in months. I catnap when I can, but as for sleeping continually for a few hours, I've forgotten what that's like."

"We can get you the help you need to combat the voices and the battle noises. Just trust me. That's all I ask of you. Trust me, Rob."

Heroic Justice

He hesitated for a moment then turned a little, his gaze fixed on his wife and children. "If I got the help I need, would you let me be a father and a husband once more, Beth?"

Lorne twisted on the spot towards Beth. Silently, she pleaded with the woman to make the right decision for her children's benefit.

Beth looked confused. Her eyes darted from Lorne to the colonel, then to her husband. As she shook her head, the sound of a gun going off made Lorne turn to face Lawton. He had dropped to the ground, and his brains covered the path all around him. Beth and the children screamed, then Katy hurried them away from the scene. Lorne rushed to see if Tony was okay. Lawton's blood had spattered on Tony's face, so Lorne took a tissue from her pocket and wiped it off. "Are you all right, Tony?"

He seemed shell-shocked when he answered. "Why? Why take his own life like that?"

"It was the voices he struggled to contend with. None of us know what it's really like to be in that situation. Constantly battling to know right from wrong. He wasn't entirely guilty for carrying out the crimes he committed. He was driven to it by his mental illness. He likely had no idea what he'd done until the voices died down, if they ever abated. From what he's just told us, I don't think they ever did. Here, let me help you stand up."

"I need my leg, Lorne."

She ran to fetch it.

Tony tried to attach the prosthetic, but something was wrong. "Damn, I think I need a new one. Can you help me to the car?"

Hero saw them struggling and rushed to help. Tony hooked an arm around Hero's shoulder.

"I've called SOCO and the pathologist, and they'll be here soon," Hero said before helping Tony to the car.

Cara was standing near Lawton's body, shaking uncontrollably despite having Hero's jacket draped around her shoulders.

Lorne walked towards her then hugged her. "Hi, Cara, it's lovely to meet you. You're going to be all right now, hon."

"I can't thank you enough for rescuing me. I thought it was only a matter of time before he killed me."

"We would have prevented him from doing that, love. I'm glad you're safe. Come on, let's get you back to the car."

EPILOGUE

The rest of the week flew past. Lorne had arranged for Beth and her children to return home. They were all still very quiet and numb after what they'd witnessed. Lorne felt sorry that the children had seen their father die that way. She sensed that they blamed their mother because they were playing her up when they got back to the house.

"They'll come around soon. There's no need for any of you to feel guilty, Beth. Let's put the onus on him serving in a war zone and having to witness his friends losing their lives. For him to carry those injuries and put up with the mental torment the way he had for months would have destroyed the strongest of wills in the end."

"I know. But if I hadn't hesitated the way I had, I can't help feeling that he wouldn't have killed himself. Why? Why do that in front of his children? I'll never be able to forgive him for that."

"I know it's hard. What's happening about the funeral?"

"It's all in hand. The funeral is going to take place next week. Will you be there?"

Lorne smiled. "Do you want me to be there?"

Beth nodded. "If you don't mind. I don't think I could handle it alone."

She patted her hand. "Then I'll come. I need to go now, if you're sure you'll be okay?"

"We'll be fine. I know the children will come around sooner or later. I'll just have to be patient."

Lorne hugged Beth and left. She was off duty, and they had the christening of Katy's daughter to look forward to, so they drove straight home. When she arrived, Lorne found Charlie showing Cindy Rayner around the kennels. Lorne had already interviewed the girl a few days ago and offered her the job of managing the kennels. She seemed wise beyond her nineteen years, and her love for dogs was evident when she made a big fuss of Sheba before she'd even acknowledged Lorne at her initial interview. Other people would have been offended by that, but in Lorne's eyes, the girl could do no wrong going forward.

"Hi, Cindy. How's it going?"

The pretty long-haired brunette smiled broadly. "I'm super excited, Mrs. Warner. Can't wait until Monday."

"Are you looking to be sacked before you even begin to work here?"

Horrified, Cindy glanced at Charlie then back at Lorne. "Sorry? Have I done something wrong?"

Lorne winked at Charlie. "I'm Lorne around here. You can cut the formality, okay?"

"Okay, I'm sorry, Mrs... I mean, Lorne. Thank you again for giving me the opportunity. I won't let either you or the dogs down—I promise you."

"If I thought that, I would never have employed you, Cindy. Carol will be here on Monday morning to show you the ropes. I'm sure you two will get on really well together."

"Thank you, I can't wait."

Lorne left the two girls alone and walked across the yard to the house. Tony was sitting at the kitchen table. He was dealing with a chronic infection in his leg due to his heroics. She kissed him and filled the kettle. "How is it, love?"

"Giving me jip. How did things go with Beth?"

"Okay, her relationship with the kids is a tad strained, but I think they're strong enough to pull through it together."

"Let's hope so. Did she mention the funeral?"

"It's next week, and I've said I'll go."

"Would it be all right if I come with you? I'd like to pay my respects to the man. None of this was his fault, Lorne."

"I know that, love. No one has any idea what someone suffering from PTSD truly goes through. Colonel Drake is delving into it further and trying to come up with a solution. Let's hope he accomplishes that soon before another case like this rears its ugly head."

"Sadly, there will always be the odd person who struggles to deal with the voices."

Lorne nodded, fearing her husband was right. Hopefully, she wouldn't have to deal with the consequences of a similar event in the near future.

THE END

Thank you for reading HEROIC JUSTICE; I sincerely hope you enjoyed reading this novel as much as I loved writing it.

If you liked it, please consider posting a short review as genuine feedback is what makes all the lonely hours writers spend producing their work worthwhile.

Heroic Justice

M A Comley

OTHER BOOKS BY M A COMLEY YOU MIGHT ALSO LIKE TO READ

CRUEL JUSTICE (Justice #1)

#1 Best-selling novel in two categories, Police procedurals and Women sleuths in both US and UK and Amazon top 20 novel.

The headless body of a wealthy widow is discovered decomposing in Chelling Forest. Then a second victim is found. Detective Inspector Lorne Simpkins and her partner, DS Pete Childs are assigned the case.

Before they can discover the identity of the killer they must make a connection between the two victims. After a third murder, Lorne receives a grisly surprise. Clearly, a vicious serial killer is on a rampage... and Lorne has become the killer's fixation.

Lorne can't allow her failing marriage or her new boss—a man with whom she shares a sensuous secret—keep her from focusing on her job. She must catch the macabre murderer, or risk becoming the next victim.

MORTAL JUSTICE (Novella)

What would you do if you saw a stranger's life in danger?

DI Lorne Simpkins and her partner, DS Pete Childs investigate a violent attack. Lorne becomes increasingly concerned when her star witness, Donna Moran, goes missing. She knew Donna was petrified, but has Donna just gone into hiding, or has she been taken by the offenders?

IMPEDING JUSTICE (Justice #2)

For eight long years, Detective Inspector Lorne Simpkins has tracked the vicious criminal known as The Unicorn. But the killer has frustrated MI6 at every turn and remained successful at Impeding Justice.

When Lorne is targeted in a trap that results in the death of her partner, the tragedy shakes her confidence to the core. Before she has time to recoup, her teenage daughter is kidnapped. More than Lorne's professional reputation rests on her bringing The Unicorn to justice.

FINAL JUSTICE (Justice #3)

A ruthless killer returns—and former DI Lorne Simpkins is forced to revisit her ugly past.

After suffering a breakdown and quitting the force, Lorne Simpkins finds herself embroiled in a MI6 covert operation to hunt down her old enemy, a sadistic and merciless criminal whose ambition is to become the world's richest man.

Lorne tracks the madman through France, attempting to thwart his plans and bring her long-time nemesis to Final Justice.

FOUL JUSTICE (Justice #4)

Detective Inspector Lorne Simpkins is back on the force. Before she can get comfortable with her new partner, newly-promoted DS Katy Foster, the two are assigned a tragic murder case that looks like a robbery gone wrong. However, when another wealthy footballer's family meets the same deadly fate within twenty-four hours, it is clear the crimes involve something far more sinister.

Keeping her focus on unravelling the complex case isn't easy for Lorne when she learns news that throws her personal life into a spin—her fiancé, M16 agent Tony Warner, is involved in a dangerous covert operation in Afghanistan.

But innocent people are dying on her patch, and someone must catch the killers. Lorne can't allow this Foul Justice to prevail.

GUARANTEED JUSTICE (Justice #5)

Retired DCI Lorne Simpkins thought she knew what she wanted when she started an animal rescue centre with her husband Tony. Although saving and retraining exploited dogs is fulfilling,

Lorne can't help but feel that something vital is missing from her life. Linda Carter is brutally raped and left for dead in an alley. By some miracle, she survives, but now she lives each day terrified by the perpetrator's final threatening words—that her sister, Fiona, will be his next victim.

The sisters decide to adopt a guard dog and contact the rescue centre. During a home check to see if the girls and their flat are suited for a German Shepherd, Lorne witnesses Linda's horrendous injuries. The young woman knows the identity of her rapist—wealthy, playboy Graham Gibson—however, the police haven't made an arrest. The shocking story turns into a life-altering moment for Lorne. She decides to become a Private Investigator, and urges the girls to let her take up their case. Little does she know that more victims will come forward to accuse Gibson of rape.

Lorne is determined to see this vicious criminal behind bars, but is anyone ever guaranteed justice?

ULTIMATE JUSTICE (Justice #6)

A ship wreck.

Dozens of bodies washed ashore.

Clear evidence that evil has made port in London.

The horrific case piques the interest of P.I. Lorne Simpkins. It doesn't take long before Lorne learns that young, helpless women are being caged and sold to the wealthy and salacious. Old wounds are wrenched open when she suspects a cover-up by the very authorities that should be keeping lawful order. Can she trust the self-serving journalist bent on making the human-trafficking ring his next big story? When her daughter is involved in a life-threatening accident, it's difficult for Lorne to keep her head in the game. But Lorne and her ex-MI6 husband, Tony, are determined to end the repulsive slave trade and bring the criminals to justice—even if it means Lorne ends up locked in a cage herself.

VIRTUAL JUSTICE (Justice #7)

Internet Dating – A Stalker's Paradise

P.I. Lorne Warner is back in Virtual Justice, the seventh instalment in the Justice series.

Heroic Justice

The body of a strangled woman draws Lorne into an intricate investigation that expands swiftly when a second innocent is murdered. A serial killer is on the loose, plucking victims from Internet dating sites. But when a third victim—this one male—is discovered, Lorne is forced to admit her worst fears... she is on the trail of a serial killer duo.

Lorne's personal life grows complicated as her sister, Jade, struggles to come to terms with their father's death. Lorne suggests drastic measures to cure Jade's grief.

The answers are out there, but will Lorne solve the crimes and find the killer before the next victim dies?

HOSTILE JUSTICE (Justice #8)

Enticed back to the police force, Lorne again teams up with Katy, her former partner. Things are no longer the same between them, though. Katy is now Lorne's superior which could prove detrimental to their latest investigation.

The crime itself is perplexing: Four small boys discover the corpse of a woman in an abandoned warehouse. CCTV footage shows the woman was abducted in broad daylight by two hooded men. When questioned, the woman's husband swears she had no known enemies and he thought she was on holiday at the time of her death.

During the investigation a personal problem unfolds for Lorne when her teenage, daughter, Charlie, attends a friend's eighteenth birthday party — with dire consequences.

TORTURED JUSTICE (Justice #9)

Revenge... some cups spilleth over.

DS Lorne Warner and DI Katy Foster are investigating the murder of a man killed with an unusual weapon. The case takes a turn when two brothers disappear within the vicinity of the murder.

Lorne and Katy quickly determine that they may be after a group of serial killers out for their own sort of justice.

ROUGH JUSTICE (Justice #10)

After two detectives are suspended, the Met is forced to return to all the cases the partners investigated. The cold case of a missing university student, Noelle Chesterfield lands on DS Lorne Warner's desk.

Because Noelle was working her way through school as a pole dancer, Lorne and her partner DI Katy Foster find themselves with plenty of suspects on their radar. However, when the leads run dry, they call in the services of an unusual ally to find the missing student and give her devastated family some peace.

DUBIOUS JUSTICE (Justice #11)

DS Lorne Warner and DI Katy Foster are called to the scene of an electrician's suspected suicide but quickly discover that they're dealing with a murder case instead.

Katy's family emergency forces her back home to be by her parent's side in Manchester, leaving Lorne as detective inspector, working alongside a new, and frustrating, partner.

When two more murders of tradesmen occur, the investigation throws suspicion on a couple who have recently renovated their home. However, the forensic team uncovers a lot more than anyone bargained for.

CALCULATED JUSTICE (Justice #12)

Let the chase begin...

Lorne Warner, newly reinstated as Inspector again, is confronted with one of her worst cases to date. She knows who kidnapped the Hardy family—their kidnapper contacted her himself. But he forces Lorne and her team into a game of cat and mouse that leads them on a chase across London.

As each clue brings Lorne closer to finding the family, she realises that saving the lives of the Hardy might mean sacrificing her own.

TWISTED JUSTICE (Justice #13) (A joint investigation between Lorne Warner and DI Sally Parker)

When the local pathologist asks DI Lorne Warner and DS Katy Foster to attend the scene of an accidental explosion, it's not long before the capable detectives find that the victim was murdered aboard his boat before the "accident" occurred.

Delving into the victim's past leads Lorne across the county border into Norfolk, where she calls upon her good friend DI Sally Parker to assist in the investigation.

What the joint team reveals about the victim's extended family blows them away. Can Lorne and Sally find the crucial evidence in time to prevent the notorious family from carrying out their own twisted justice to sustain their wealth?

PRIME JUSTICE (Justice #14)

A killer, an abductor, and a villain intent on revenge — just a normal week in the life of DI Lorne Warner.

When a wealthy woman is found murdered in a country lane, close to her home, it's up to Lorne to find the evidence to track down the rural killer.

When another resident in the same vicinity is abducted, the evidence points Lorne to believe both cases are connected.

However, Lorne's focus on the puzzling case is in jeopardy, when a criminal awaiting trial threatens her career in the force.

Can Lorne restore the tranquillity in the once sleepy community? And will she still be a serving police officer in the Met by the end of the investigation?

HEROIC JUSTICE (Justice #15)(A joint investigation between DI Lorne Warner and DI Hero Nelson)

One Killer. Several gruesome murders. Two hundred miles apart.

This case is going to take two exceptional detectives to solve it. DI Lorne Warner and her husband, Tony, travel north to team up with DI Hero Nelson, on the trail of a killer randomly killing his victims in public places.

It soon becomes apparent the killer is toying with the detectives. To stay ahead of the investigation team, he changes his MO and ups his game... with a devastating outcome.

BLIND JUSTICE (a Justice 20,000 word novella and prequel to Cruel Justice)

DI Lorne Simpkins and DS Pete Childs are called to investigate the death of Jenny Bartlett, who's decomposing body is found in a wooded area. When Lorne informs Jenny's parents of her death they are understandably shocked but also confused by the news as they were under the impression their daughter was out of the country, working as a volunteer in Africa.

Delving deep into Jenny's personal life leads Lorne to Jenny's former boyfriend, Simon Killon, after Lorne discovers they had a secret liaison in a restaurant shortly before her death. But is he guilty of Jenny's murder?

After learning what traumas Simon himself has encountered lately, Lorne has her doubts that he's the culprit. However she finds it hard to disprove the evidence pointing in his direction.

MORTAL JUSTICE – a 12,000 word novella.

A 12,000 word Justice short novella to be read between CRUEL JUSTICE and IMPEDING JUSTICE from NY Times and USA Today bestselling author M A Comley.

What would you do if you saw a stranger's life in danger?

DI Lorne Simpkins and her partner, DS Pete Childs investigate a violent attack. Lorne becomes increasingly concerned when her star witness, Donna Moran, goes missing. She knew Donna was petrified, but has Donna just gone into hiding, or has she been taken by the offenders?

IRRATIONAL JUSTICE – (a 10,000 word short story)

A fast-paced short story thriller in the bestselling Justice series.

Heroic Justice

In a race against time, with the life of a young woman at risk, DI Lorne Simpkins and her partner, DS Pete Childs find themselves in an impossible situation which puts them in mortal danger.

Can the dynamic duo rescue her before she draws her final breath, or will they fall victim to a diabolical killer?

JUSTICE AT CHRISTMAS – A Justice short story.

A Christmas short story of 10,000 involving all the old members of the team.

DI Lorne Simpkins and her partner DS Pete Childs encounter a dangerous gang of Santas who plan on creating havoc on the streets of London on Christmas Eve.

Pete is persuaded to go undercover to foil the gang's audacious plan.

WRONG PLACE (DI Sally Parker thriller series #1)

DI Sally Parker has a serial killer on her patch. One thing that sets this killer apart from the others she's hunted before: his willingness to leave DNA at each of the crime scenes. It's up to Sally and her partner DS Jack Blackman to find out why before the body count rises to double figures.

While Sally is engrossed in the investigation, her ex-husband, Darryl, pays a surprise visit to her new home. His actions not only threaten Sally's new-found confidence, but they also force the DCI to give Sally an ultimatum concerning the case.

Can Sally overcome all the obstacles fate has placed in her path and arrest the brazen killer?

NO HIDING PLACE (DI Sally Parker thriller series #2)

The discovery of Gemma Whiting's bludgeoned body within spitting distance of her family home, opens a new case for DI Sally Parker, one that quickly embroils her in Gemma's feud with male family members. The more Sally digs, the longer her suspect list grows.

Frustrated after months of investigation, yet another young woman is attacked close to where Gemma's body was found. Sally begins to wonder if she's been looking in the wrong direction for the killer.

COLD CASE (DI Sally Parker thriller series #3)

DI Sally Parker has been handed a ten-year-old cold case. However, the victim, Aisha Thomas, isn't just a member of the public—she's a serving police officer's wife.

During the original investigation, the suspects disappeared before they could be questioned. Now fresh evidence has been uncovered, proving the two suspects to be innocent. Sally has to start over at the beginning. She uncovers a few surprises that were either overlooked. . . or purposefully ignored by the original investigator.

When the case threatens Sally's fledgling romantic relationship with pathologist Simon Bracknall, she begins to suspect someone is determined to hinder her chance at happiness—as well as solving Aisha's murder.

Is Sally getting close to revealing the killer or has she stumbled across something even more sinister?

DEADLY ENCOUNTER (DI Sally Parker thriller series #4)

Murderer or a victim of a corrupt system?

Fifteen years after her deadly encounter, Anne Gillan's remains are finally found. Her husband, who has maintained his innocence, has spent those fifteen years in prison—and the case's investigating officer has been found guilty of corruption. Could Anne's murderer still be free?

DI Sally Parker has just been chosen to lead a cold-case squad—and Anne Gillan's murder is their first case. The case brings Sally face to face with a criminal from her own past, who has set out to destroy Sally's relationship with her soon-to-be husband.

Will Sally and her team solve the case before Sally has a deadly encounter of her own?

WEB OF DECEIT (A DI Sally Parker novella)

DI Sally Parker is called to one of the best hotels in the area after one of the guests, Megan Carmen, reports her friend, Tina, missing.

Sally investigates Megan's background when the woman reveals that she has just arrived from France and Tina is a woman she met on the Internet. Do genuine people truly arrange to innocently meet people they've only just met online? Or, in light of Tina's disappearance, is there something far more sinister afoot?

CLEVER DECEPTION (co-written by Linda S Prather)

A 20,000 word introductory novella to TRAGIC DECEPTION

"Have you ever watched the light fade from someone's eyes, Foxy? The pigment slowly, ever so slowly disappear?"

The press call him the Escape Artist, and he is certainly living up to his name.

Sergeant Alexandra Fox has never come up against such a devious mind in her entire career. Ten young women, seven of them wives of fellow officers, have been found tortured and murdered. Every tiny lead fizzles out, and he revels in taunting them by phone, torturing them mentally as he forces them to listen to the screams of his victims.

Alexandra, is determined to catch him before he kills again, unaware that she's become the object of his obsession until he issues one last threat: "I thought I would give you one warning. A chance to back away and leave the investigation. Don't make me punish you."

TRAGIC DECEPTION (Book one in the Deception series co-authored by Linda S Prather)

"Seek liberty, Foxy, and you'll find me."

Sergeant Alexandra Fox came to America to find the man who had brutally murdered her sister. A man the press called The Escape Artist. Could a British Sergeant fit in with the NYPD? Not if Commander Patterson had anything to do with it.

Suspended with only two friends in America— Chief Brown, a long time family friend, and retired Sergeant Matt "Nobby" Adams,

Alex has seven days to find three kidnapped babies, or look for a new job.

Her investigation leads her into a world of deception, that turns tragic before it even begins, and a helping hand from the one person she hated the most—The Escape Artist.

SINFUL DECEPTION (Book two in the Deception series co-authored by Linda S Prather)

"At the end of the day, Foxy, we're not all that different, really. I'm going to enjoy working with you."

Detective Alex Fox now had positive proof that The Escape Artist was not only in New York, but monitoring her every move. As a member of the newly formed Special Investigations unit of the NYPD, she's finally in a position to find him, put an end to his villainous crimes and avenge her sister's brutal murder.

When the mutilated bodies of three teenage runaways are recovered, and with the abduction of former Commander Patterson, Alex is forced to put her plans on hold, as the unit is called in to investigate these horrendous crimes. With the two cases running side by side, Alex and her team are stretched to the limits in this edge-of-your-seat thriller.

FOREVER WATCHING YOU – A DI Miranda Carr thriller.

With everything to live for, wealthy cosmetic entrepreneur Anneka Morton is on the cusp of launching a brand-new range of products... but her husband reports her missing just days before the launch party.

When intrepid Detective Inspector Miranda Carr arrives at the crime scene, the clues indicate that Anneka was abducted from her own home. Without a body, she suspects foul play from a cosmetics competitor. However, DI Carr's case gets turned on its head when Anneka's body is found, and the last person Miranda suspected goes on the run.

Miranda hops on a plane to Portugal with her boss, DCI Caroline Gordon, and enters into a joint covert operation with Interpol to arrest and extradite Anneka's murderer.

EVIL IN DISGUISE – Based on True Events novel

Caught in an abusive marriage, Jenny Slater desperately hopes there is more to life than the lies she tells to hide the bruises. Her three children have no idea their father is a monster, and Jenny struggles with the decision to tell them of her torment, which she can no longer bear alone.

Jenny's pen pal in the States is the only person aware of the truth.

When Helen pleads with her to visit, Jenny is undecided about leaving England when her family is at odds. However, when a letter from a mysterious source arrives, seeking Jenny's help, she flies to the States. Her attempts to save another trapped soul only entangle her in another manipulative relationship.

TORN APART (Hero series book #1)

Everyone understands about the no-go districts—areas of the city so overrun with gang violence even the police stay away. In this book, the first in a new series, DI Hero Nelson sets out to combat the issue.

When Saskia Hartley and her nine-year-old son are run down outside a restaurant, DI Nelson knows it is no ordinary hit-and-run incident. He's looking at a homicide case... and the evidence points to the brutal Krull Gang. When two prostitutes are murdered, but little interest is given to the women on the Krull's payroll, Nelson connects the dots.

DI Nelson has to decide whether he's dealing with a turf war or something far more sinister.

END RESULT (Hero series #2)

Before DI Hero Nelson has the chance to get used to his new role as a father to brand-new twins, a murder investigation steals his attention. When a second victim is discovered on his patch, Hero has his eye on a single perpetrator for both murders — but the suspect has a solid alibi for both crimes.

Hero continues his investigation until he obtains a surprising end result.

IN PLAIN SIGHT (Hero Series #3 published by Bloodhound Books)

No one is safe... not even the police.

DI Hero Nelson is used to violent crime but this one is personal. When he's called to a crime scene he discovers the victims are two police officers one of whom is a good friend.

Determined to track down the killer, he's dealt another blow as the body count continues to rise. To catch the killer before he strikes again, Hero calls upon the public for help. But when the criminal ups the ante by taking hostages, he soon regrets his actions.

Can Hero and the police catch the murderer before more innocent victims are hurt?

Hero must apprehend a killer who is hiding in plain sight before the time runs out.

DOUBLE JEOPARDY (Hero series #4 published by Bloodhound Books)

Successful entrepreneur, Ross Spalding, has everything to live for; a thriving business, a stunning new home, and a high society wedding to his beautiful fiancée to look forward to in the coming months. That is, until his life comes to an abrupt, gruesome end.

DI Hero Nelson and his team need to dig deep to find the reasons behind someone wanting Ross Spalding dead. As more people connected to Ross also die, some in suspicious circumstances, the suspect list grows beyond all expectations, until a major clue presents itself and spins the investigation off in a totally new direction.

However, Hero's personal life is also dealt a major blow when his parents are faced with a life or death situation. He is forced to put his personal problems aside when the murderers are revealed and Hero is faced with a tight deadline in which to apprehend them.

DEADLY ACT (A Hero series novella)

When Hero's wife is involved in a car accident with her best friend in which the driver left the scene, he decides to investigate the case. Hero soon discovers that Nelda has had to contend with a string of strange things happening to her since she broke off her engagement to Paul Fox.

Can Hero pin any of the strange events on Paul before he carries out his final deadly act?

SOLE INTENTION (Intention series #1)

Former police officers Ellen Brazil and Brian Lynx have joined forces to start a successful missing persons investigation firm which has just been contracted to find the wife of bodybuilder Will Endersbe. Ellen discovers that a number of women with similar features and hair colour have also vanished in the Worcester area. Ellen and Brian suspect a serial kidnapper is to blame, and without a body, the police are happy to leave the case in their hands to solve.

Hoping the women are still alive, Ellen digs for clues and races to find the women, despite her troubled private life and a meddlesome stepfather with a violent secret.

GRAVE INTENTION (Intention series #2)

Private investigator Ellen Brazil is hired to find ex-banker Charles Dugan, who disappeared after his mansion burned to the ground. Ellen quickly discovers that Dugan's new profession—playing poker full time—has earned him a circle of very dangerous "friends."

Ellen's investigation is disrupted when her mother is injured, leaving Ellen to wonder why her mother's abusive husband has gone missing when he should be at the hospital. Ellen finds herself trying to solve two cases at once while smoothing over her own personal issues.

When she learns Dugan has plans to flee the country, Ellen knows it's imperative to find him before the gang he owes money to discover his whereabouts and carry out their grave intentions.

DEVIOUS INTENTION (Intention series #3)

The stakes are high when a holiday turns tragic...

When Louise Gillespie regains consciousness after a traffic accident, she learns that her husband and four-year-old daughter are missing. Her frantic search to find them is encumbered by her own brain trauma and the local sergeant in charge of investigation, who thinks she's crazy.

Her luck finally changes when she bumps into PIs Ellen Brazil and Brian Lynx. Despite being on holiday themselves, they take on Louise's case. It's not long before Ellen and Brian discover the truth behind the family's sinister disappearance.

THE CALLER (The first gripping novel in the Organised Crime Team series co-authored with Tara Lyons)

When The Caller rings... what would you do?

The Organised Crime Team is a newly-formed unit with one of the toughest tasks in London. Led by DI Angie North, their first investigation is a cold case that has foxed several officers in the Met for months.

After Angie holds a TV appeal regarding the case, a number of similar aggressive attacks are brought to her attention. The team call on their contacts on the street for help. Their interest is sparked when several local names surface.

To bring the criminals to justice a member of the Organised Crime Team is asked to risk their life in a dangerous covert operation.

It's A Dog's Life

This is a 12,000 word novelette that takes place between Cruel Justice and Impeding Justice and is based on actual events.

It may not be homicide, but to DI Lorne Simpkins it's still murder.

When a reporter friend of DI Lorne Simpkins gives her a tip about a story involving ex-racing greyhounds, Lorne is sceptical.

But after delving into it, she's horrified to discover the grisly fate of racing dogs that are no longer useful to their owners—and she's determined to bring the cruel and uncaring owners to justice...

"Animal welfare is so close to my heart, the real-life plight of these former racing dogs moved me to tears. I'm delighted to donate all profits of the book to PUPS, The Protection of Unwanted Puppies Society."

Merry Widow

This is a 5000 word short story to accompany the best-selling Justice series.

It's just an ordinary day in the life of D I Lorne Simpkins until she gets a phone call from a woman whose husband has died in unusual circumstances.

Lorne takes up the case with disastrous results for both her and her partner DS Pete Childs.

PAST TEMPTATION (a Temptation novella)

Until now, Nicole's main focus in life has been running her successful business while raising her daughter, Sammy Jo, single-handedly. Now, Nicole's ex-boyfriend, Josh has turned up determined to rekindle the relationship he ran out on.

Before they get the chance to pick up where they left off, Nicole's personal life is put in mortal danger.

A Romantic Suspense novella. 25,000 words.

LOST TEMPTATION (a Temptation novella)

Chrissy fears she is losing her boyfriend, Kyle, so she formulates a plan to try to get their relationship back on track.

However, events drastically backfire when a car chase puts both their lives in danger.

A Romantic Suspense Novella 20,000 words.

A Time To Heal (a Romance novella)

Family Liaison Officer, Chloe Fullerton is helping hero pilot, Captain Steve Ewing, recuperate from injury after he landed his stricken plane, avoiding a major disaster.

Chloe's sworn off love ever since she lost the love of her life. But the spark between her and Steve makes her feel she may yet love again. There's turbulence ahead though—Steve's ex-wife is determined to wreck his and Chloe's blossoming relationship.

Novella approx 33,000 words.

M A Comley

A Time For Change (a Romance novella)

Based on a true story.

Danielle Pires's life is going well. She has a boyfriend who wants to marry her and is building a reputation as a talented and hard-working interior designer. Keen to expand her portfolio, Danielle is delighted by a request to breathe life back into the Victorian Mansion that handsome Scott Jordache is renovating.

Her parents, meanwhile, have organised a surprise Caribbean cruise to give her a much-needed break.

Danielle sets sail only to discover Scott aboard the same ship, but mysteriously travelling under a pseudonym. Intrigued, she feels torn between mistrust and being drawn in by his charm.

Should she let herself fall for Scott or return to the security of the man she left at home?

33,000 words.

Printed in Great Britain
by Amazon